Jeff looked down the street to the dark towers of the medical compound. "The Hoffman Center," he said softly. "He got into the Center, somehow. He must have."

"But that doesn't make sense," Barney said. "That's no public treatment unit. That's their main research laboratory. The place they do their experimenting. And from what I hear, they don't welcome visitors there. If he went in there, they'll throw him out on his ear any minute."

"Or else they'll throw him to the Mercy Men," Jeff said.

Barney stared at him in horror.

Hi dd fick

I read this a long time ago
and thought you might like
it. I'd even like to re-read
it. so when I saw it the
other day in the book-store
I thought I recognized the
title - Good Reading

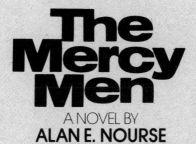

# The Mercy Men

A NOVEL BY

**ALAN E. NOURSE**

ACE SCIENCE FICTION BOOKS
NEW YORK

FOR

ELINOR AND BUZ BUSBY

AND NOBBY TOO.

THE MERCY MEN

An Ace Science Fiction Book / published by arrangement with
David McKay Co., Inc.

PRINTING HISTORY
This edition / June 1984

An earlier, briefer version of this book was originally published by
Ace Books under the title of *A Man Obsessed*.

ISBN: 0-441-52561-X

Ace Science Fiction Books are published by The Berkley Publishing Group,
200 Madison Avenue, New York, New York 10016.
PRINTED IN THE UNITED STATES OF AMERICA

## Part One

## THE HUNTER

### I

THE PLACE was cheap and dirty and smelled bad, just about the scurviest-looking dive Jeff Meyer had ever seen in his twenty-one years, and he had seen plenty of them lately. Huddled at a table in the rear, the youth clutched a glass in his hand and tried to dodge the glare of the ever-shifting lights. The reek of bad liquor, cheap perfume and sweat brought tears to his eyes, but he shook his head doggedly and peered through the smoky haze toward the big circular dance-bar at the far side of the room. Then, for the tenth time in as many minutes he looked again at his watch, fighting down a wave of panic.

Something was wrong. Barney should have been here an hour ago. And he knew he had to have Barney's help when Conroe came.

It was early yet, not even ten o'clock, but already the place was crawling with the evening's clientele: drunks, bar-girls, drifters, seedy-looking long-haired types with their vague-eyed girls, a sprinkling of the really sick ones sitting around in stupor as if waiting and listening for something that never quite appeared. A three-piece band behind the bar shifted into a shock-beat number and Jeff tried to close his ears to the sudden deafening noise. He wished right now that he could be somewhere else, *anywhere* else, far away. He didn't belong in a place like this. He never had. But he couldn't leave, not now, after waiting so long for this one evening.

Because Conroe would be coming here within another hour, and the trap was set. It was not the first trap he and Barney had set for Conroe in these past three years, not by a long shot, but this was going to be the last one. Always before, Conroe had spotted the trap, somehow, and gotten away. Not this time. Jeff was certain of that.

This time there was no place for Conroe to hide . . . no place at all.

Across the room the bar was already crowded with dancers caught up in the hypnotic shock-beat of the band. Hysterical laughter burst from a group over to the right, and a stuporous drifter at the next table stirred and muttered something unintelligible. In spite of himself, Jeff looked at the man: the scrawny neck, the sagging jaw, the idiotic unearthly expression of intent listening on the sallow face. Nothing new about it, of course; the country was full to overflowing with human wreckage like this lately, but Jeff still had to fight down a wave of shock and revulsion whenever he saw one of these vacant faces close-up. There were too many sick ones like this, these days, too many ruined minds in worn-out bodies, too many people suddenly turning strange without warning, abandoning homes and jobs, drifting the streets, and ending up in places like this, never to return. Far too many for the hospitals to hold or the doctors to treat, and more turning up every day. . . . Jeff tore his eyes away, searching the room again. *What was keeping Barney?*

Carefully, he reviewed the events of the last few days. With the help of the girl, Barney had finally spotted Conroe again, after that last debacle, holed up in a cheap hotel across the river. Barney had bugged the room and set up a round-the-clock stakeout while Jeff worked with Barney's crew and, indirectly, with the girl, to set the trap. Tonight Conroe was to meet her here after her first show; he and Barney would cover the place inside, while their men sewed up the streets and alleys outside. Jeff shivered; all that was very fine, but Barney should have left before dark to join him . . . where was he? He wished now that he had dealt with the girl directly, at least had a look at her, but the men had assured him that she would play along.

"Take a trip, mister?" The bar-girl had a tray slung at her waist and gave Jeff her most enticing smile.

"Get lost," Jeff muttered.

The smile faded. "I was only asking," the girl whined. "You don't have to—"

"I said *get lost*." She was blocking his view, and he twisted to see around her, his apprehension growing every second as more people crowded into the place. He didn't hear what she snarled at him as she moved away; he was too busy trying to focus on faces. He couldn't afford a slip-up this time. The trap was perfect, it *couldn't* fail. They'd learned a lot about Conroe in these three years of hunting . . . about his personality, his habits, the things he did, the places he went, the few friends he made. Last time it had been Jeff's own blundering error that had let the quarry slip the net at the last moment, and Conroe had vanished as completely as if he had died. But then at last Barney had found the girl, and through her traced Conroe again, and this time Jeff knew it was the end of the road. If this chance were lost, there might never be another.

At last he saw a small, gray-haired man making his way back toward the table. Jeff sighed his relief, until he saw the worried frown on Barney Trimble's face. The man sat down across from him. "Sorry I'm late," he said, "but there was nothing else I could do."

"What's wrong?" Jeff said.

"Something's funny," the older man said. "He left the hotel an hour ago and went to a telephone booth, even though he has a phone in his room. Made three calls that we couldn't tap. Then right back to the hotel again. He was still there when I left."

"You didn't leave him uncovered?"

"No, of course not, but something doesn't smell right."

Jeff leaned fiercely across the table. "Barney, believe me, *this had better not go sour tonight.*"

His friend regarded him wearily. "Get hold of yourself," he said. "You look like you're about to fly apart. Even if Conroe *did* happen to come here tonight, he'd spot you in no time, this way."

Jeff's hand trembled as he sank back in the chair. "What do you mean by that?"

"I mean this is ridiculous. He isn't going to show."

"He'll show," Jeff said softly.

"How do you know? You've got nothing but a paid informer's word for it."

"The girl is here, isn't she?"

"Oh, yes. No doubt about that."

"And she talked to him last night?"

Barney nodded. "We both listened in on the calls."

"Then he'll be here, and we'll get him," Jeff said. "The girl is too scared to cross us up."

"But what if she's even more scared of Conroe? What if something else goes wrong? Suppose you lose him again . . . then what?" Barney held up his hand to cut off Jeff's reply. "Oh, I know, it can't possibly go wrong. I'm not supposed to talk like that. I'm not supposed to ask questions, or say anything you don't want to hear. But I can't sit around and watch you tear yourself apart like this much longer, boy. You've been chasing this man for three straight years now and something has always gone wrong, every time. What are you going to do if it goes wrong again? Jeff—*what's it worth?* Suppose it happens to go right, suppose you nail this man tonight, what are you planning to do then? What do you want of him?"

"You know what I want of him," Jeff said.

"You want to talk to him," Barney said sourly.

"That's right. Just talk to him."

"And what else?"

"I . . . I don't know what else."

"You're a liar." Before he could move, Barney's hand was in Jeff's jacket pocket, hauling out the heavy stun-gun and dropping it on the table top with a thud. "You could kill a man with that little toy if you happened to hit him right, don't you know that? Did you think I didn't know you had it? Well, I'm no fool. I've stuck with you right from the start of this thing, but I'm not going to be a party to any murder."

Jeff Meyer was shaking his head. "You're wrong, Barney. I don't want to kill him. At least I don't think I do. I just want to talk to him. Find out *why he runs*. Find out why he did what he did to my father." He took a deep breath. "I've got to know that. Conroe has been haunting me for half my life, and I've never even so much as had a good look at him. Maybe he haunted my father for years before that. I don't know. But I've *got* to know."

"You didn't even know Conroe existed until three years ago."

"No, but he was there all the same, buried in my mind for years before that, and I've got to know why. If I have to stun him out cold and strap him to a chair to find out, I'll do it. If I have to bribe somebody at the Hoffman Center to pick his brain in order to find out, I'll do that too. They're handy enough, their labs are just down the block from here and they aren't too fussy what they do around that place, either, from what I hear. You've heard about the Mercy Men. Well, I don't care what it takes or what it costs, I've *got to find out* about Paul Conroe."

For a moment the older man just stared at him. Finally he sighed and tossed back the gun. "Okay," he said. "Whatever you say. You're too old for me to wipe your nose any more. But there's one thing you'd better know, Jeff. I've stuck with you because you asked me to, and because I was your legal guardian for ten years before this started. I couldn't be more worried about you if you were my own son. But for three years now I've watched you disintegrate right in front of me, toss aside your education, spend a fortune of your father's money and tear yourself apart piece by piece, all on account of a blind obsession that you yourself don't even understand. Well, maybe you can go on like this, but I can't. I've had it. If something goes wrong and you don't get Conroe tonight, I'm through."

Jeff nodded, feeling numbness creeping through him, as though something inside him had died. He had known it would come to this, sooner or later. He couldn't blame Barney. He couldn't even deny what Barney said. He knew how much he had changed in these three years even better than Barney did. He knew what this thing was doing to him . . . the grinding tension and the snarled nerves, the bitter lines around his eyes and mouth, the erosion of values he had once thought important, the hard core of anger and frustration and— yes, admit it—blind rage that had been building up inside him day after day.

Jeff Meyer knew he didn't belong here in a skid row dive; he belonged back in the college classes he'd left, working for the engineering degree he once had yearned for. He had no use for the giddy, half-hysterical people crowding these smoke-filled holes night after night, trying frantically to escape the driving pressure of their days in the city. He hated the stench of these places, cringed at the howls of forced laughter, shrank from the stuporous drifters who haunted the bars and then retired to their strange, unearthly dream worlds. This was a world *Conroe* had dragged him into, but he knew he couldn't stop now, no matter how much he wanted out.

He leaned back in his chair, trying to force his tense muscles to relax. "Take it easy, Barney," he said gently. "Nothing's going to go wrong. I'll get Conroe tonight. But if not this time, then the next time, or the next. With you or without you. I'm sorry, but that's the way it has to be."

By now the place was packed. The band ended a number; dancers drifted back to their tables, and an MC walked out on the bar with a traveling microphone. Then the lights dimmed and a huge red spotlight caught the curtain at the back of the bar. Jeff saw Barney lean forward as the crowd hushed; the curtain parted and a girl stepped forward to a fanfare of tinny music and took the mike from the MC's hand.

"That's her," Barney said.

"Are you certain?"

Barney nodded. "No question about it. Conroe's supposed to meet her here after this show." He glanced around the room carefully. "I'd better move to the other side before she spots me," he muttered. "Watch yourself." He slipped silently away from the table.

The girl was nervous. It showed in her face and in her voice the moment she started singing. Her face was attractive—almost beautiful—except for the fear in it, the strange, haunted look as her eyes searched the room. Her hair was long and black, flowing down around her shoulders, and she moved with grace to the music, but the smile on her lips was purely for show and the song sounded as if it were coming from a mechanical doll.

The music quickened, with a hypnotic under-beat that sent a chill down Jeff's spine. There was tension in the room; even the crowd seemed to sense something wrong. The song shifted, too, and then the girl's eyes met his momentarily and widened slightly. Her voice seemed to falter for an instant. Recognition? Impossible. She'd never seen him before. And yet. . . .

Suddenly she swung down from the bar, still singing, mike still in hand, and began moving casually from table to table. Jeff felt the tension rise in the crowd around him, sensed the eagerness and desperation in their eyes as they watched this lovely girl. Her smile was more relaxed now, the fear seemed to be gone, and she moved with confidence as the spotlight followed her, playing tricks with her hair and gown. Jeff sat rooted as she moved closer and closer, approaching his table. And then, before he could move, she was across from him, turning to him with a mocking laugh and pointing her hand toward him as the red spotlight hit him full in the face.

"*Get out of the light!*" Barney yelled from across the room.

Like a cat Jeff shoved his chair back and hit the floor, knocking the girl aside as he went. There was a scream, and the light swung to the girl, then back to him. The table went over; he rolled away from it and twisted to his feet, fighting his way through the screaming crowd. The stun-gun was in his hand as he paused, searching the room—

"*Get him! There he goes!*" Jeff swung to the sound of the voice, and his eyes caught the movement of a tall, slender man lurching away from the bar. There was no mistaking the face of Paul Conroe, the hollow cheeks, the high forehead, the wide prominent eyes. It was a face Jeff had seen in his dreams a thousand times, the twisted, frightened face of the man he had been hunting for three long years. For an instant Conroe crouched there, staring at him; then he was gone like a ghost, swallowed in the crowd as he made for the door.

"Stop him!" Jeff roared to Barney. "He's heading for the street. *Get him!*" He sighted the stun-gun over the bobbing heads, then fired wildly at the moving man, felt the gun jar his hand as the microwave charge went crackling about harmlessly from wall to wall. A scream rose at the shot; people dropped to the floor to get out of the way, glasses crashed, tables went over. Someone was clawing at Jeff's leg, trying to bring him down, and then, abruptly, all the lights went out.

"Outside! he's out through the door!" It was Barney's voice now, over the uproar. Jeff plunged to the side of the room, wrenched open the emergency exit he had spotted when he first came in, and ran down the narrow alleyway to the street. Half a block away he saw a tall figure running pell-mell, down toward the looming buildings of the Hoffman Medical Center compound at the end of the street. A car slid away from the curb in pursuit of the fleeing figure—one of the men Barney had staked out to close the net if Conroe got out of the building. Jeff stopped, panting, as Barney came up behind him.

"He can't go anywhere," Barney said. "There are men on every corner with cars and spotlights."

"But where is he trying to go?" Jeff raged. "That girl —that miserable, two-timing girl—she sold us out! She put that spotlight on me the minute she saw him come in! But he must *know* the streets are blocked. *Where does he think he's running?*"

"I don't know. There's nothing open in this whole block but this place and the Hoffman Center, and he can't get out of the block. Our cars will either grab him or drive him back."

They stared down the gloomy street, waiting. Jeff's hands were shaking beyond control and his shoulders sagged in exhaustion and defeat. So close, *so close*. But down the street now, no sound, no movement. The nightclub door burst open as people peered out, nervously, buzzing with excitement. Jeff and Barney stepped back into the shadow of the alley. In a few moments the buzzing died down and the crowd went back inside, half relieved, half disappointed.

In the silence Jeff and Barney waited. Five minutes passed, then ten. Nothing. Finally a car turned the corner and one of Barney's men came up to them. "Get him?" the man asked.

"No. What about the others?"

"Not a sign. He never reached the end of the block."

"He *must* have," Jeff said, "unless he got through to one of the back streets."

"No chance of that. Those streets are sewed up tight," the man said. "Even so, I'll check." He stepped to the car radio, spoke briefly, then came back shaking his head. "Nothing there."

Jeff stared at Barney, unbelieving. Then, suddenly, he looked down the street to the dark towers of the medical compound beyond. "The Hoffman Center," he said softly. "He got into the Center, somehow. He must have."

"But that doesn't make sense," Barney said. "That's no public treatment unit down there. That's their main research laboratory. The place they do their experimenting. And from what I hear, they don't welcome visitors there. If he went in there, they'll throw him out on his ear any minute."

"Or else they'll throw him to the Mercy Men," Jeff said.

"They can't do that. The government outlawed the Mercy Men years ago."

"Sure. Of course they did. There's no such thing as the Mercy Men nowadays—except for the rumors that say they're still there."

Barney stared at him in horror. "Look, Jeff, Conroe may be desperate, but he hasn't lost his wits. People who volunteered for the Mercy Men didn't come back."

"Some of them did. A few. Some even came back rich, the way I heard it."

"Yes, with their brains turned into scrambled eggs, as a special bonus." Barney Trimble shook his head. "Jeff, use common sense. Even if they *did* exist. Conroe would never take a gamble like that."

"He might, if he were scared enough. And they'd take him in, too. They wouldn't ask any questions, they'd just swallow him up. Above all, *they'd hide him,* and I don't think they'd care too much just why he wanted to be hidden."

"He'd have to be insane," Barney muttered.

"Not necessarily. Look at it from this point of view. He knows I've been hunting him for years. I don't know why he keeps running, but *he* knows why. He also knows that I'm not going to quit, and that sooner or later I'll win. He's running out of luck, Barney. Every time we've missed him it's been a little closer than the last time. Well, you add it up. A man can run and hide just so long, and then he begins to run out of hiding places. But if he's desperate enough to take the risk, the Mercy Men could be a last resort, the best hiding place of them all."

They stood together in the darkness then for a long time, shivering in the cold wind that whirled down the alley. Far overhead a westbound jet broke the silence with its cry and a gyro-car whispered by on the street like a prowling animal. Somewhere in a Hoffman Center tower a light blinked out.

Finally, Barney sighed. "Well, if you're right and that's where he went, then your hunting is over. There's no point even worrying about it any more. He's dead, and that's that. Not one in a thousand ever came out of there. Even if the rumors are true, you might have to wait for years, and then not even recognize him."

Jeff Meyer straightened up sharply. "Sorry," he said, "but I can't wait for years." He looked at his friend. "Now listen to me. Keep your men staked out for the rest of the night, just on the chance that he's found a hiding place somewhere out here. Get some of them to comb the roofs. We can take the alleys ourselves. If he's out here, we'll find him."

"And if he's not?"

Jeff smiled. "Then I know where to look for him, don't I?"

"But if he's gone in there, he's *gone!* There's no point chasing him any longer."

Jeff peered through the darkness at his old friend, half angry and half sad. Poor Barney . . . it wasn't any good, even now, to try to explain. Faithful as he was, after all these years Barney still didn't understand. Jeff reached out, touched the older man's shoulder gently. "You've been a wonderful friend," he said. "More of a

15

friend than you know. But I have to find him, you see.
There's nothing else I can do."

"But *where?*" Barney cried.

"Wherever he's gone," Jeff said. "And if that means I
have to go into that God-forgotten place after him, that's
where I'm going to go."

## II

LONG HOURS of darkness came and went, and then a
gray dawn, with a misty drizzle that wet the streets
and pressed down on the city like a leaden blanket.
The little car radio brought bits and snatches of morning
news, in between the toothpaste ads. ". . . casualties are
still mounting in central London this morning as the
noise riots continue into the eleventh day. Most May-
fair area streets remain blockaded in spite of yesterday's
British troop assault. However, a Government spokes-
man stated this morning that the riot cycle had already
crested, according to statistical analysis, and predicted
that complete order would be restored within another
week. On the domestic scene, the stock market rallied
yesterday from a three-week nosedive on strengh of
Government rumors in New York Sector that the con-
troversial new tax increase would not be enforced. And
in Philadelphia Sector, Hoffman Medical Center spokes-
men announced another 5% increase in the Mental Illness Index this month, the largest monthly increase in
over two years. . . ."

Jeff Meyer sat in the car with Barney, only half-listen-
ing. Then he snapped off the radio with a snarl. For
hours during the night he and Barney had searched
through the alleys while the other men combed the
neighboring rooftops. Now the last man drove up to

report. "No good," he said, spreading his hands. "Not a sign of him."

"Well," Barney sighed, "I'm afraid that's it, then."

Jeff nodded. Along the street morning traffic was picking up, and cars were beginning to fill the parking tiers across from the Hoffman Center administration building. On both sides of the street the other buildings of the great medical complex rose, level upon level, their white marble façades disappearing in the low-lying mist. It was an immense complex of buildings, this central research unit that served the ever-growing medical needs of an overcrowded country and world. Elsewhere there were Hoffman Center hospitals and outpatient treatment units, hundreds of them now, all over the world. But this was the very heart of the Hoffman Center, sprawling across six perfectly landscaped city blocks, with tall trees and cool green terraces setting off the proud rise of the towers.

Now, at the foot of the towers, a buzz of activity had already begun. Supply trucks were moving up to the unloading ramps, bringing food and supplies, medicine and equipment, for the twenty-two thousand people these buildings housed—doctors, nurses, lab technicians, engineers and patients alike. Only special patients whose illnesses required special equipment, special care, special study. High in the tower wards, thousands of doctors conducted careful clinical studies, hundreds of laboratories were busy day and night, engaged in every imaginable type and variety of research and study in medicine, psychiatry, biochemistry, genetics. . . . FOR THE BENEFIT OF MAN, the familiar slogan said.

And beyond any question, the slogan was true. The Hoffman Medical Center, in all its immensity and with all of its research and treatment facilities, was a dream finally come true, the last and greatest step in the age-long search for ways to conquer human illness, fight death and relieve pain. A century before, research in medicine had been carried out in thousands of independent centers, disorganized, uncoordinated, inefficient. Treatment of illness around the world had varied in quality all the way from the splendid to the barbaric. As knowledge grew, even the problem of disseminating knowledge to the doctors who needed it had become insurmountable.

In fact, the Hoffman Medical Research Center had first started as a mere computerized clearing house for medical knowledge. Later it had become a center for medical training, then grew and blossomed as a vast, world-wide treatment, research and training organization, crossing all national boundaries, serving the needs of all faiths and races. Finally, just twenty-five years ago, this central research headquarters had been designed and the cornerstone laid. Even those who had conceived it had not realized the immensity of the need it would fulfill. No expense had been spared in building it; the world's finest architects had designed the high-rising ward towers, the gleaming façades, the laboratories and archives and computer rooms reaching as far underground as the ward towers were high. Equipment unequalled in the world was installed in this Center's dressing rooms and surgeries, and the doctors and nurses and researchers and technicians who staffed the Center came there from every country in the world. As the acknowledged leader in the world of medicine, the Hoffman Center had never failed in its leadership.

But Jeff Meyer was not thinking about that now, as he peered down the foggy street toward the glass doors of the administration building. He was thinking of other, darker activities concealed somewhere within that great pile of buildings, and of a man who had vanished there. He stirred and looked over at Barney. "You'll cover things for me out here?"

"Of course. But Jeff, this is crazy."

Jeff forced a laugh. "Don't worry about it. Just wait

until you hear from me. And you *will* hear from me. I won't let anybody box me in." He hoped he sounded more confident than he felt.

Barney sighed. "Okay. But give me that stun-gun before you go."

Jeff hesitated, then handed over the gun. "Guess it won't be much help in there anyway," he said. He shook Barney's hand, one final tight grip. "Believe me, I'll be okay."

"Good luck, then. You'll need it."

With one last nod, Jeff climbed out of the car and snaked his way through the traffic, hurrying down the street toward the huge glass doors. He knew his old friend would be waiting there for a while, hoping he would change his mind, but he didn't look back.

He simply didn't dare.

Inside the vast lobby he paused and stared about him with a mixture of awe and apprehension. He had never been inside a Hoffman Center building before, although he had heard of the Center's activities innumerable times. The public had never been welcome here, except for those applying for the minor voluntary jobs still permitted by law since the Mercy Men had been formally outlawed. Curiosity-seekers were actively discouraged, but the newspapers and television never tired of reporting stores of the vital and sometimes heroic work that was done behind these walls. Every day brought glowing reports of progress in medical research, of new discoveries made, of new medicines becoming available. But there were other stories, too, that did not come from the newspapers . . . stories passed by word of mouth, whispered scare-stories accompanied by nervous laughs and sneering cynical jokes, rumors and remarks ascribed to aides or technicians who worked at the Center, or tales told by wide-eyed drifters in the bars and alleys. Not the kind of stories anyone would care to believe, Jeff reflected, but hard stories to forget or ignore.

Across the lobby an elevator came down from one of the towers, discharging half a dozen white-garbed women in nurses' caps. A man in a white lab jacket ran to catch the up car, stethoscope dangling from his side pocket. Jeff sniffed uneasily. There was a slightly distasteful odor in the air, an aura of almost unbearable cleanliness and spotless preservation. For all its huge size and cathedral-like stillness, the lobby was a center of unceasing activity. Elevators came and went, interbuilding jitneys terminated here, and people kept coming from one place and going to another, moving briskly, never slowly, always with an air of grave importance.

Carefully Jeff looked around, spotting the corridor leading to the main administrative offices, the jitney and elevator locations, the strategic positions of the watchful, gray-uniformed guards. Almost instinctively he tried to print an indelible picture of the layout of the building in his mind, for future reference, because somewhere in here he would find Paul Conroe. Somewhere in this maze of buildings and passageways, the man he had hunted for so long had vanished during the night. Logic told him that; every other alternative had been exhausted. Jeff's muscles ached from the night-long search and his eyes were red from sleeplessness, but he felt a hot, angry glow of satisfaction just to know that Conroe *had* to be here, and from here there would be no more escaping, if the grim rumors were true.

"You have business here, mister? Or just snooping?"

Jeff whirled around and nearly crashed into the burly man in the gray uniform. He forced a grin. "Yes. I mean, no. I'm just not sure where to go."

"Then maybe you should go back outside." The guard eyed him with suspicion.

"But I'm looking for the volunteers' desk; the ad in the paper said there were openings for people with AB blood."

The guard grunted. "Okay. You want the Administration Office." He pointed across to a corridor marked *Research Administration*. "Right over there, first door to your right. The nurse inside will take care of you."

Jeff started toward the corridor as the guard continued to watch him. It was public knowledge that a few volunteers were taken on to assist in blood grouping studies, new drug analyses, serum fractioning experiments and other innocuous things. The Center paid volunteers well for their time and the minor discomfort of the tests, even advertised, sometimes, when a new study was starting.

But this was not the program Jeff was interested in. It was not where Conroe would have gone to escape him. He had no real evidence that the program he was looking for even existed at all; certainly the Center didn't advertise it. All he had to go on were rumors and reports: stories of drunks stumbling into Hoffman Center emergency rooms and never coming out; tales of swift, silent raids on narcotics houses in which the captured ones never reached any police station; tales of discreet word-of-mouth advertising among the dregs of society, the ones who were down and out, with promises of unimaginable wealth if certain necessary services were performed well and if the volunteers were lucky. Once Mercy Men had worked here, open and aboveboard, as human guinea pigs in vital but extremely dangerous research programs, until such practices were banned by law as inhumane. If the rumors were true and such programs still existed, they would be cloaked in secrecy and highly illegal. But if that were the case, how could he contact the right people? Jeff glanced down at his unpolished shoes, rubbed a finger over his purposely unshaven chin. How would they screen a volunteer who wanted a chance at the big money? What would they do if they found out he was a fraud, an interloper? He shivered as he faced the office door. It would be a gamble, a dangerous long shot, for if there were Mercy Men here, they would not have much patience with an outsider coming in to snoop around.

He would have to become an insider, or appear to.

He glanced back, saw the guard still watching him. Then he pushed open the door marked *Volunteer Registration*. It opened into a small waiting room. Several people were sitting along the wall. Across the room was a desk with a nurse behind it, enclosed in a transparent privacy booth. A mousy-looking man with a bald head and dishonest eyes was sitting opposite the nurse in the booth, talking to her as she busily filled out a card for punching. The man was angry, gesticulating, but no sound came from the plastic enclosure. It was like a scene from a movie without any sound track.

Finally the man got up and left, and a middle-aged woman moved up to take his place at the desk. The nurse hadn't even looked up when Jeff walked in. He took a seat, fidgeted, glanced at his watch. . . . Must she be so slow? Nothing seemed to hurry the woman, she worked from person to person, unruffled, impersonal, with a fixed, chilly smile on her lips. At last she looked up at Jeff with a cool nod, and he moved to the chair inside the booth. "Name, please," she said.

"You don't have a card on me."

She looked up briefly. "A new volunteer? Fine. Then we'll ask you to fill out a data card. If you'll give me your name, I can start—"

Jeff cleared his throat, felt a pulse pounding there. "I'm not just sure what I want to volunteer for," he said cautiously.

The nurse looked at him. "There are several programs you can choose from, you needn't decide this moment. We have regular antibiotic runs on Tuesdays and Thursdays. You take the drug by mouth in the morning, and give blood samples at ten, two and four. Those runs pay thirty dollars plus your lunch while you're here. Or you you could give blood for serum fractions, but you'd be restricted to once a month, and that only pays twenty dollars, no lunch. Or—"

"You don't understand," Jeff broke in. "I want *money*. Lots of it." He looked straight at her. "I've heard you have other kinds of work."

The woman's eyes narrowed. "Well, there *are* higher-paying studies, of course, but they rarely accept new volunteers. You must understand that they pay more because they involve substantially higher risk to the volunteer's health. But of course, you can always apply. Circulation studies involving heart catheterization pays as much as a thousand dollars, sometimes, but usually we start—"

"I said *money*," Jeff interrupted. "Not peanuts."

For the first time the woman really *looked* at him, took in his bleary eyes and unshaven stubble. It was a long, penetrating stare. Her smile was gone completely now, and her fingers were suddenly nervous. "Do you have any idea what you're talking about, young man?"

"I'm talking about the Mercy Men."

She sat silently for a moment, still watching him. Then her lips twitched with disgust and she stood up. "Excuse me, please." Abruptly she disappeared through an inner office door. She was gone a long time. Jeff waited, trembling, aware of the sweat on his forehead but too tense even to fumble a handkerchief out of his pocket. He avoided the eyes of the others who were waiting, staring at him accusingly for taking so much time. Then the nurse reappeared at the inner door. "Come in here, please.

*Then he was right!* Jeff tried to conceal his excitement as he took a seat in the small anteroom the nurse indicated. She went to a phone on the desk, punched a number code. The silence was almost intolerable as she waited for an answer, a silence so thick he could hear her breathing. Finally a signal light blinked and she took up the receiver. "Dr. Schiml? This is the Volunteers' Desk, doctor. I'm sorry to bother you again, but

I have my instructions." She shot Jeff Meyer a swift glance. "There's another man up here you'll probably want to see."

## III

LATER, as he waited alone in the anteroom, Jeff wondered if he could possibly have misheard her. She had continued talking on the phone for a moment in a cool, matter-of-fact tone: "No, he hasn't given a name, doctor . . . that's right, he just now walked in . . . quite young, early twenties . . . yes, I know that, doctor, but he was quite specific. . . . Very well, then, I'll have him wait." She hung up the phone. eyeing Jeff as if he were some kind of biological specimen, and walked out without another word.

Jeff stood up, stretched his legs, and examined the room. It was small, with just a desk and two or three chairs, obviously a consulting room of some kind. One wall held a panel of push buttons, some sort of an input-output device tied into a central filing system somewhere, he assumed. On the desk was the telephone with its closed-circuit TV screen and camera; over the screen a lighted panel announced the date in sharp black letters: 23 April 2109, and below it the little transistor clock had just changed to read 9:25 A.M. Half the morning gone already, with his quarry drawing farther away with every passing minute.

He waited impatiently, staring out the window at the rising tiers of buildings. Across the courtyard the first of the ward towers rose, and to the left was a series of long, low buildings with skylights: kitchens, perhaps, or some other kind of maintenance buildings. Dozens of buildings, any one of which could be hiding Paul Conroe. Jeff clenched his fists, then consciously forced himself to relax. This was no time to get tied up in knots. He *might* know where in the building Conroe was but the doctor who was coming to see him knew for sure. Jeff knew he'd heard the nurse correctly. *"There's another man you'll probably want to see."* And that could only mean that one man had come in recently; as recent as the middle of the night, for example.

A door opened behind him, and Jeff turned sharply. The man who came in closed the door again, carefully, and walked over to the desk. He looked up at Jeff, smiling.

"My name's Roger Schiml," he said pleasantly. "I direct some of the research we do here. And you—I understand you wanted to talk to me." He looked at Jeff squarely.

Jeff nodded. "That's right. I just came in to ask—well—just to talk to you," he finished lamely. He felt a sinking feeling growing in the pit of his stomach as everything he had planned to say seemed to leave him, crumbling away like dust. This man hardly looked like a doctor, although his white jacket was immaculate, and the inevitable stethoscope stuck out of his side pocket. He was tall, and slender, perhaps fifty years old, with round, cheerful pink cheeks and a long sad nose that gave his face a droll expression. A harmless-looking man, Jeff thought, except for his eyes: blue eyes, very blue, the sharpest, most penetrating eyes Jeff had ever seen. Those eyes were watching him more carefully than Dr. Schiml's smile seemed to indicate, watching Jeff's every move, studying him. The eyes were full of wisdom; they were also tinged with caution.

The doctor sat down facing Jeff and offered him a cigarette from a case on the desk. Jeff shook his head. "No thanks," he said, "I don't use them. Anyway, I thought they were slightly illegal nowadays."

The doctor grinned. "Slightly. Thanks to us, as you probably know. We were the ones who finally got tobacco on the proscribed list." He leaned back easily in his chair, stuffing a pipe and lighting. "Still, a smoke sometimes helps gets things talked out. Settles the nerves, they say. By the way, I didn't get your name."

"Meyer," said Jeff. "Jeffrey K. Meyer."

The doctor smiled. "I hope Miss Finch didn't bother you too much. She handles most of the new volunteer applicants here, you see. But in special cases she turns the interview over to me." He paused. "Cases like yours, for instance."

Jeff blinked, his mind racing. It was going to take acting, real acting to fool this man. The doctor's face was deceptively open and benign, almost complacent, but the eyes were far from complacent. They were old, old eyes that had already seen far more than eyes ought normally to see. To fool a man with eyes like that—Jeff took a deep breath. "I want to join the Mercy Men," he said.

For a long moment Dr. Schiml said nothing, just stared across at him. Then he said, "That's interesting. It's also very curious. That particular term, I mean. Oh, I can understand why certain people might be attracted to medical mercenary work, all right, but the name they use for it has always baffled me. Mercy Men. Very picturesque. Makes you think of scenes from bad movies —handsome young interns fighting against death, brave heroes giving their all for the good of humanity—that sort of garbage." The eyes hardened. "Where did you hear about the Mercy Men, I wonder?"

Jeff shrugged. "It's an open secret, doctor. Everybody's heard about the Mercy Men. Of course, you don't advertise in the newspapers, any more, but every skid row bum knows that there's big money waiting here for anybody who wants to take the risk."

Dr. Schiml looked him straight in the eye. "Suppose I told you that no such organization exists any longer, here or anywhere else?"

A tight smile appeared on Jeff's face. "I'd call you a Class-A liar."

Schiml's eyebrows went up. "That's a big word. Can you back it up?"

A memory suddenly came into Jeff's mind. "You bet I can. I *know* there are still Mercy Men here. I talked to one of them, not more than three months ago. He was a drifter with a taste for morphine when I first ran into him—he had a champagne appetite to go along with a beer income. Then he disappeared for about six months, just vanished completely. And when he turned up again a few months ago he had a big fancy place up in the Catskills and more hard cash than he knew what to do with. Of course, he uses all that money to feed several hundred cats down in his basement—" Jeff looked up. "He never cared for cats much, before he disappeared, and he's funny in other ways, too. Nothing serious of course, just—peculiar. But he doesn't seem to need drugs any more. And he's very rich."

Schiml smiled and put his fingers together. "That would be Luke Tandy. Yes, Luke *was* a little different when he left, but the work he did was satisfactory, and we paid off."

"So I hear," Jeff said. "Three hundred and fifty thousand dollars. Cash on the line, for him or his heirs. Or the cats, if he doesn't have any heirs."

"So what are you doing here?" Dr. Schiml asked suddenly.

"I want three hundred and fifty thousand dollars, too."

"Rubbish," the doctor said.

Jeff reddened. "What do you mean by that?"

"I mean don't try to lie to me," Dr. Schiml retorted. "I'll catch you every time." The doctor's eyes were hard. "What kind of a fool do you think I am? I sit here and look at you, and I see a strong, healthy, intelligent young man—very intelligent and very young—who hasn't missed a meal in his life. Okay, so you've missed a night's sleep, and you haven't shaved for a day or two; so what? You're wearing dirty clothes, but you paid good money for them when you bought them. You obviously don't drink. You obviously don't use drugs. You're obviously strong and mentally competent. And then you tell me you want to join the Mercy Men for money. So you lie. I'll ask you again: what are you here for?"

"For money. For three hundred and fifty thousand dollars."

The doctor sighed and leaned back. "All right, you decline to answer. It isn't important, at this point. Something else is, though: *what sorts of risk are you prepared to take?*"

"Whatever risk is necessary," Jeff said softly. "As long as the payoff is right."

"All right; then let me tell you something," Schiml said, "and I think you'd better listen. It wasn't any public outcry that got the Mercy Men banned by law fifteen years ago; the Hoffman Center practically begged to have it legally banned. And it isn't any accident that your information about the program is so vague. We've been very careful to keep it vague. The more vague the stories, the fewer snoops and thrillseekers and busybodies we have to contend with. The more distasteful the stories that we spread around, the more desperate people have to become before they turn up here. And this, above all, is what we want. Because the work we are doing requires very desperate people for volunteers."

As he was talking the doctor had opened a desk drawer and pulled out a pack of cards. He began riffling them in his fingers. At first Jeff ignored them; then he saw the faces of the cards, and he felt something suddenly tighten in his chest.

They were curious cards, not regular playing cards at all. The faces carried peculiar markings, simple symbols in scarlet and white unfamiliar to Jeff, yet he found himself shivering and tense as he looked at them. He shifted in his chair, trembling, forcing himself to pull his eyes away. "Desperate," he echoed. "You were saying you wanted desperate people."

Dr. Schiml leaned back, giving the cards a final riffle and tossing them down on the desk. "Exactly. The more desperate, the better. We've done some very important work since the Center opened—work based on many years of background research. A century ago doctors were fighting some terrible medical problems. Hepatitis was a killer then. So were pneumonia, heart disease, cancer. All those diseases are beaten now, modern doctors never even see them any more, but as the old killers were driven back, new ones moved in. Look at the neurotoxic virus plagues we've been having, appearing out of nowhere fifty years ago, and still not beaten. Look at the drifters you see in every bar today, a completely new kind of pressure-and-panic psychosis that we haven't even been able to describe very well yet, much less cure. Look at the statistics on all kinds of mental disease, rising in geometric progression almost every year."

The tall doctor stood up and walked to the window. "There, in particular, the Hoffman Center is concerned. We don't know why it's happening, we don't even know for sure *what* is happening to people's minds, but *something* is happening, something vicious. Something that has to be stopped." He picked up the cards, riffled them again, and dropped them into his pocket. "That's one of our jobs—to find out what this creeping illness is, and to find out how to stop it. But we can't even find a lead until we know a lot more than we've ever known before about the human brain and how it works the way it does. We don't even fully understand the *structure* of the nervous system yet, much less how it functions. And we've learned all we can learn, by now, from studying cats and dogs and monkeys. Further study of monkeys might teach us more about monkeys, but it

won't teach us what we need to know about *men—*"
He paused, looking at Jeff. "I think you can see what
I'm getting at."

Jeff Meyer nodded slowly. "You need men," he said.
"That's right. Men to study. Men to experiment with,
frightful as that may sound. We can't learn what we
need to know from any other kind of—experimental
animal. But there are problems. You go fooling around
with a man's brain, and he's likely to die on you, quite
abruptly. Or he may suffer irreparable damage, or go
insane. We plan our work well, but no matter how careful we are, we can *never* be sure of results. Some of
the results are pretty horrible. Your friend in the Catskills was one of the lucky ones. But we're making
progress. Not very fast, but progress. Right from the first
we had to have volunteers, the right kind of volunteers.
Nobody in his right mind would volunteer for such
work without incentives, so we provided incentives. For
the most truly altruistic work in the world, our workers
come to us from the most mercenary of all motives: we
pay for their services, and we pay well. Three hundred
thousand dollars tax-free is a small fee, by our standards. Some jobs pay millions; we have every government in the world behind us, and the sky is the limit, if
we need a particular man for a particular job. The fee
is paid when the job is finished, either to the volunteer
or his heirs. It isn't nice work, and we don't find nice
people applying. You can see why the name they've
given themselves is so strange: Medical Mercenaries,
the Mercy Men. You can also see why we want them
to be desperate before they come here. More desperate
than you are, from what I can see."

Jeff Meyer stared at his hands, waiting in the silence
of the room. His eyes strayed once again to the curious
cards, and again, strangely, he felt his chest tighten. It
was no news, what Dr. Schiml had said. This was a port
of last resort, a road that could end in horror or death.
Barney Trimble said it wasn't worth it; Conroe would

never escape alive, anyway, he had said. But Jeff knew that Conroe could. To follow him here was insane, a terrible risk, but somehow the risk didn't matter now. Already he had thrown aside the life he had planned, spent three years hunting a man down like a cat in the jungle, following Paul Conroe to the port of last resort. Nothing else in his life had mattered, these three years. It had been a long, grueling hunt, tracking the man, following him, studying him, tracing his movements, setting up trap after trap, until Conroe had become desperate enough to come here rather than face Jeff. Why? Jeff didn't know why. All he knew was that he had become desperate too. In spite of what Barney said. In spite of anything. Like it or not, he couldn't stop now.

*And if he isn't here, Jeff? What about that? What if he slipped you and never came here at all?* It had been gnawing his mind all along, and he thrust the thought back angrily. *He's here. He has to be here. Another man came here, before I did.* Jeff looked up at the doctor, his eyes hard. "I haven't changed my mind," he said. "What do I do to join?"

Dr. Schiml sighed, and turned to the file panel. "There's no guarantee that we'll even want you," he said. "We need people with certain particular qualities; others we can't use at all. You'll have to be tested thoroughly before we'll know. We'll also have to have proof of your age, but that's easy enough to determine during testing. Meanwhile, you'll be confined in a pre-assignment ward, and you'll obey the rules governing those wards. You won't like the rules, and you won't like the company, but that's your headache, not mine. One false move and you'll be out on the street; it's all up to you."

"And if I pass the testing?"

"You'll get a job assignment, and sign your release and you're in." The doctor leaned forward, punched a number on the viewscreen, and picked up the telephone. He tapped idle fingers on the desk as a face fluttered and came clear on the screen. "Blackie," he said tiredly, "better send the Nasty Frenchman up here. Looks like we've got another new recruit."

The visiphone snapped off. Jeff sat frozen to his seat, his heart suddenly pounding. Dr. Schiml was saying something to him, but he didn't even hear him; his eyes were still fixed on the darkened viewscreen. For just a moment, the face on the screen had been clearly visible: a woman's face, with large gray eyes, framed by blowing black hair. It was a face Jeff would never forget: the girl he had seen the night before, singing in the red spotlight.

## IV

THERE WAS no question, it was the girl in the nightclub, the singer with the flowing hair, who had led them to Conroe and then sold them out. Jeff fought for control as Dr. Schiml watched him with a puzzled frown. "Its nothing," Jeff said, "just nerves, I guess," but inside a voice was crying out, *"He's here! Conroe's in here somewhere!"*

But why was *she* here? Schiml had called her "Blackie," spoken with familiarity. Jeff's mind whirled. He had the sudden strange feeling that he had missed something, somewhere along the line, something he sensed but couldn't quite grasp. What could it mean for the *girl* to be here?

Or had her appearance at the nightclub been the unusual one?

A buzzer rang, and the office door opened to admit a small, weasel-faced man. The doctor looked up and smiled. "Hello, Jacques. This is Jeff Meyer, a new recruit. Take him down below and get him quartered in on 17-D; all right? And you may brief him a little on the way down. He's awfully green."

The little man scratched his long nose, and regarded Jeff coldly. "A new one? Not a special one, I hope. Too many waiting in line already."

"No, nothing special. We'll see where he tests out, first. Then if we can use him, we'll talk jobs. Meanwhile, he needs to learn the rules. You can teach him."

The little man's face cracked into an unpleasant smile, revealing a row of dirty yellow teeth. "You bet, doc. You know me." He stared critically at Jeff, and the grin broadened. "A big one, too, big as Harpo. But I guess they fall just as hard as the rest. Want me to take him right down?"

Schiml nodded. "Maybe the commissary's still open. He hasn't eaten." His eyes turned to Jeff. "This is Jacques," he said. "They call him 'the Nasty Frenchman,' but that's just a joke, of course. He's been around for a long time, he can show you the ropes. And don't let his sense of humor bother you too much. As I say, he's been around a long time. You'll be assigned quarters, and you'll stay with your own ward group for meals and recreation, everything else. . . . That means no contact outside the Center as long as you're here. You'll get the daily news reports, and there are magazines and books in the library. If you've got any business anywhere else you don't belong in here." He paused for a long moment and gave Jeff a strange look, almost a half-smile. "Oh, yes, one thing: questions don't go over very well around here. Any kind of questions. Asking questions can make you very unpopular."

The Nasty Frenchman shuffled his feet nervously, and Jeff started for the door. Then the little man turned back to Dr. Schiml. "They brought Tinker back from the table about ten minutes ago. He's in pretty bad shape. Maybe you should look at him?"

"This was the big job today, wasn't it?" Schiml's eyes were sharp. "What did Dr. Gabriel say?"

"He said no dice. It was a bust."

"I see. Well, it may just be the anesthetic wearing off now, but I'll be down to see what I can do."

The Nasty Frenchman grunted and turned back to Jeff. His face still wore the unpleasant smile. "Let's go, big boy," he said, and started down the hall.

## V

JEFF DIDN'T know where "down below" was, but apparently it was a long way down. Certainly not up in one of the bright ward towers, as he had imagined. Jeff followed the weasel-faced man, counting corridors as they passed, trying to keep himself oriented. He glanced at his watch impatiently. Minutes were slipping by, minutes that could mean success or failure to him. There were a dozen questions going through his mind now, things that didn't quite add up, but central to all of them was the girl. She was the key, somehow. She would know where in these tunnels and corridors Conroe could be found.

They reached an elevator, stepped aboard, and shot down so fast Jeff clutched at the rail. They went a long way down; his ears popped twice before the car stopped and the little man led him out into a well-lit corridor. Glowing light panels in the walls made the hall as bright as daylight, but cast no shadows. The Nasty Frenchman went to a call box and punched buttons; in a moment a jitney car on an overhead monorail swung into view and dropped down to receive them.

"In," the little man said.

The car was cramped for two, but Jacques worked the controls with one hand. The car rose to the ceiling and took off, swinging crazily as it sped along through a maze of corridors and curves. They passed people along the way: nurses, doctors, orderlies pushing patients on wheeled stretchers with intravenous bottles strapped to poles on the corners, a few men and women in the same blue dungaree fatigues Jacques was wearing, an occasional gray-clad guard with holstered stun-gun. Jeff stirred uneasily, growing more and more confused with every turn. "Look," he said finally, "where's this thing taking us?"

The Nasty Frenchman grunted. "You worried or something?"

"Well, it looks like we're headed for the center of the Earth. I'd like to be able to find my way out sometime."

"Why?"

The question was so blunt that Jeff's jaw sagged for a moment. "Well, I'm not planning to spend the rest of my life in here."

The Nasty Frenchman chuckled. "You're not, huh? Just in for a nice restful vacation, I suppose. Well, you wise guys are all the same. Go ahead and dream." He turned his attention to the controls again and the car swung sharply to the right down another corridor. Jeff scowled, watching cross-corridors flash by. Were they really going so far down? Or was this just an illusion, a deliberate scheme to lose new recruits so completely in this huge place that they could never find their way out unaided . . . or thought they couldn't? Jeff shrugged. It really didn't matter, too much. He had a job to do, and it had to be done here. He would worry about escaping when the time came.

He looked briefly at Jacques. "That girl," he said, "the one the doctor called Blackie, is she down here where we're going?"

"How would I know?" the little man said. "I don't have a leash on her."

"Well, no; I just wondered if she's one of the group—one of the Mercy Men?"

The Nasty Frenchman ignored the question. He threw

a switch, and the car swerved down a long side corridor. In the dim light his face looked pasty yellow, wrinkled and bitter. With his mat of stringy brown hair, he looked exactly like a mummy; the effect was hideously intensified when he grinned. Jeff watched him for a moment or two, then tried again. "Have you been here long? With the Mercy Men?"

"Yeah."

"How'd you happen to come here?"

The Nasty Frenchman looked at him. "Look, did I ask you why you were here?"

"No."

"Then don't ask me." He ignored Jeff for a few moments. Then: "Take some advice. Just shut up and fit in, as fast as you can. Don't ask questions, just do as you're told. You'll share a room, and you'll eat at seven, noon and six. They'll start testing you when they get ready, and they want you in your room when they come for you. They'll also want you alive; some recruits don't even make it to testing. They have accidents or something." He grinned. "Until you're tested and assigned and signed your release, you're nothing around here. If you make it through testing, you may be lucky and get a good assignment. Some of the work is with central nervous system, some is with autonomic systems, some concentrates on spinal cord and peripherals, but mostly these days they're interested in the brain proper. That pays the best, too—quarter of a million at a crack, with a fairly good risk."

"What do you consider a good risk?"

Jacques shrugged. "Maybe ten per cent full recovery. That means complete recovery from the work, no secondary infection, complete recovery of all brain functions, so that you come out good as new. A *fairly* good risk job has more casualties, maybe only five per cent recovery. A bad risk job averages one or two per cent recovery at best." The little man grinned at him. "Matter of fact, you'd have a better chance living through a firing squad than some of those jobs. And once you sign your release, relieving the hospital the doctors of all responsiblity, you're bound by contract and there's no way out. Of course, now, if you're lucky enough to come through—" For the first time the little man's eyes seemed to come to life, bright with avarice. "If you come through, they pay off. Oh, how they pay off! You can go away rich for life. If you're lucky you'll get a good job for a starter, make maybe a hundred grand with hardly any risk at all." He paused, regarding Jeff closely. "Of course, there are incomplete recoveries, too. Sometimes the doctors have trouble keeping them out of the news, if they ever leave. Pretty messy, too. Sometimes."

Jeff realized the man was baiting him, taking a perverse pleasure in his reaction to these horror stories, all the more cruel because they were undoubtedly true. Was he running this jitney around in circles just to prolong the torture? Jeff closed his mind to the thought. Maybe so . . . but what did he expect to find here? Kindness and consideration? What kind of man would be down here at all? Had Jacques been a different kind of a man before he came here? How long had he been here, waiting from experiment to experiment, waiting to live or to die, waiting for the payoff, for the staggering wealth that might be his at the end of a job? What would such a life do to a man? *Nothing good, Jeff. Nothing good at all.*

Sharply, the car turned a corner and dropped down to a stop. The Nasty Frenchman hopped out, motioned to Jeff to follow. At the end of the hall was an escalator; Jeff searched each doorway they passed, alert for a sign of the black-haired girl. "To get back to Blackie," he said finally, "I didn't know they had any women in this set-up. Who is she?"

The Nasty Frenchman stopped in his tracks. "Say, what is this?" he said. "She an old family friend or something, you keep asking about her?"

"I just know her from somewhere, that's all."

"So why bother *me* with your questions?"

Jeff's face darkened angrily. "I want to see her, anything wrong with that? Don't get so jumpy."

The little man whirled on him like a cat, pinning Jeff's arm behind his back until he felt the tendons pull. With unbelievable strength Jacques twisted him back against the wall, glaring up at him. "You're a smart guy, you are, coming around here asking questions," he snarled, giving Jeff's arm a vicious wrench. "You think you're fooling me? You ask about this, you ask about that, about Blackie, about me. . . . Why so nosey? *What are you doing here?* Going for the money or asking questions?"

"The money!" Jeff gasped. He fought to break free of the ironlike grip.

"Then don't ask questions! We don't like nosy people here, we like people who roll clean dice and mind their own business."

The little man gave Jeff's arm a final agonizing wrench and released him, jumping back, poised and eager, begging Jeff to charge him. Instead, Jeff slumped against the wall, rubbing his aching arm and fighting for control. A fight now would ruin everything; already he'd blundered badly. He swore at himself under his breath. Even without the doctor's warning he should have known that people in a place like this would not tolerate snooping. And now word would surely get to the girl that he was asking questions about her. . . .

. . . if he didn't get to her first.

He turned to the Nasty Frenchman, still rubbing his shoulder "Okay, forget it," he said. "I won't ask questions. Now where do we go from here?"

# VI

THE ROOM was small and bare, with sterile-white walls and stainless steel chairs and bed. Immaculate but depressing, it merely added to Jeff's gloom. He walked in with the Nasty Frenchman at his heels, and stared at the two stark hospital beds against opposite walls, the two foot lockers, the two small desk-and-chair combinations. There was no window, just glowing light panels in the walls and a forced-air ventilator. In fact, there was nothing about the room or corridor to prove that they were not twenty miles underground, and certainly the jitney ride had been no assurance to the contrary. The walls were newly painted and the floor was covered with clean Never-Wear plastic matting. Against one wall was a TV set; at the far side a door led into a compact lavatory and shower. Glancing in, Jeff saw that the lavatory was also connected with the adjoining double room.

"It's no Grand Hotel," the Nasty Frenchman said sourly, "but it's clean and it's a bed. This corridor quarters your whole unit: 17-D. Other units are on other floors, up and down."

Jeff looked around the room gloomily. "What about food?"

"The mess hall's four flights down—take the escalator at the end of the hall. It closes in half an hour, so you'd better not fool around. And if you're smart, you won't go off exploring on the way, either. These boys in gray you see scattered around like nothing better than to break the skulls of people they find in places they don't belong." The little man started for the door, then paused. "Just one tip," he said, "out of the kindness of my heart:

change clothes before you go down to eat. The faster you stop looking like you're new here, the happier you're going to be." And with that he turned and disappeared down the hall.

Jeff gave a sigh, and prowled the room. One of the foot lockers held an amazing assortment of clean and dirty clothes. Its floor compartment was stuffed with dirty shirts and trousers, and nested squarely in the center of the pile was a heap of gold rings and wrist watches. Jeff blinked, not quite believing his eyes. He hadn't thought to ask about his roommate, but apparently he had one who wasn't around at the moment. The other locker had clean shirts and dungarees; he started to change clothes. His muscles ached all over, and he felt dry and scratchy-eyed from lack of sleep. The arm that Jacques had twisted ached miserably every time he moved it. More than anything else he wanted to sleep for a little while—but that would waste still more precious time. At least in the mess hall there would be people around, and somewhere among them he might spot the girl.

Carefully he considered the problem. First he had to find the girl, and quickly, before she had a chance to alibi or hide. Conroe would surely be hiding; he would never come into the open until he was sure that he had not been followed. And he too must be taken unawares. If Conroe had time to plan he might slip away, even here.

A car buzzed down the corridor and stopped a little way from Jeff's door. He heard voices, hushed, yet oddly strident. Jeff paused, listening to a combination of unfamiliar sounds—a grunt, a low curse, a rustle of whispered conversation, a low whistle. Then the door to the adjoing room banged open and he heard the rumble-squeak of a wheeled stretcher.

"Jeez, what a job!"

"Yeah, it don't look good. Did the doc see him?"

"Not yet. He said he'd be down."

"Gotta let the dope wear off before anybody can tell anything, I guess. He really had the works, this time."

Jeff walked quietly to the door of the connecting lavatory and listened. Then he wished he hadn't. A new sound was present, a faint sound of labored, gurgling breathing. Jeff shivered; he had heard a sound like that only once before in his life, during a riot in Chicago, when a man had been hit in the throat with a chunk of shrapnel. Carefully he pushed the door open an inch, peered through.

There were three men standing in the room, maneuvering the patient from the stretcher onto the bed. The man's head was covered to the shoulders with bandages. A patch of blood showed fresh near the temple, and a rubber tube emerged where the mouth should have been.

"Got him down? Better get the blanket tighter. And the restrainers, he may jump around. Doc said it would take three weeks for shock to wear off, if he makes it through the night."

"Yeah. And this is the big money for Tinker, too. I heard that Harpo nearly had the assignment, but Schiml had already promised Tinker he could have it."

Jeff shuddered. This, then, was one of the Mercy Men, finished with a "job." The gurgling sound grew louder and softer with the man's breathing, short, shallow, a measure of death. An experiment had been completed. . . .

Jeff closed the door silently. His face was white in the mirror, and his hands were shaking. Here was the thing he had known from the start, but hadn't really faced: he was on a one-way road. He had to find Conroe, and get off the road fast. It would be insane to travel too far.

*But it's insane to be here at all* the face in the mirror said back to him.

No, not insane. He had to find Conroe, that was all. *But why? What is it worth? Why do you have to find*

41

*him? You didn't even know he existed until three years ago!*

*I didn't know, except for the dreams, but he had existed just the same. And then one day . . . one day. . . .*

He remembered how it had started, as clearly as yesterday. A wet, blustery day three years before, cold and miserable What had he been doing? Oh, yes. Crossing the campus to the library, with a newspaper over his head for shelter, because it was raining as if the whole sky were coming down. Head into the wind, he was almost to the library steps when he saw the man come out the door and walk past him—a tall, gaunt man, huddling against the rain in a gray tweed hat. Jeff saw his face, and their eyes met for an instant in passing, and Jeff stopped dead, frozen, his heart hammering in his chest. He stood rooted there, unable to move as the rain ran down his neck and drenched his clothes and filled up his shoes and the newspaper fell apart in his hand and dropped in wet gobs to the ground. . . .

And in his mind, one wrenching, searing thought: *that man killed my father. He . . . killed . . . my . . . father.* There was no doubt, no hesitation. He *knew*. Not some other man who looked like that one, not someone of that size, that build, that appearance . . . but *that man*.

Panic had seized him then. It was irrational, impossible, crazy—he had never seen the man before. He had only the vaguest childish memories of his father, long ago when he was a small boy. He had *never* known how his father had died, or why, under what circumstances. How could he have? He'd been eight years old at the time, and his father had been far away.

But now, in this downpour, his mind was not asking how he knew. He *knew*, that was all that mattered. He whirled in the rain, croaked out a shout as the tall figure hurried around the corner of the building across the campus. He broke into a run, rounded the corner himself moments later, but the man was gone. A girl in a bright raincoat came by; he grabbed her by the lapels, nearly knocking her off her feet: "Where did he go? *Quick,* I've got to find him!" She pulled away, staring at him, and he shoved her aside, raced to the nearest building, tore open the door and stared at the empty corridor. Like a madman he crossed to the next building, as a passing car almost knocked him down. Nothing was clear after that; the downpour increased as he ran, skin-soaked, first one way, then another, searching for the tall lean figure. One place he slipped and fell face-first in the mud, then cursed wildly as he picked himself up and ran on, half-blind.

Then later someone had him tight by the collar and he focused on the bland, not unkindly face of the campus cop: "Hold it, son, relax, quiet down. Get your breath and tell me what's wrong." In the cop's car he told him, but it sounded wild, he knew it sounded wild, something about killers in gray tweed hats and a long-dead father, and he struggled to get out of the car but the cop hauled him back firmly. "You can't go running around like that, you're soaked through. You need to see the doc. I'll even take you there. Bet you've got a hundred and four fever. . . ." Jeff shook his head, then stopped and nodded numbly. Maybe so. He'd had a bad cold, lots of coughing that morning. Now the cold, wet day began to look real again, not blazing red, and he was getting his breath back. Back to reality.

But the man, that had been no delirium. He remembered the gaunt face, the prominent eyes. And deep in his mind was the cold, unshakable conviction: *whoever he was, he killed my father. He was the one, no other.*

He did have a fever, they found, and an X ray showed early pneumonia. For five days he was grounded in the infirmary before he begged his way out, promising on his word that he'd rest in the dorm for another week. He'd called Barney and Em the first night. "No, not pneumonia, just a chest cold; no, don't come down, there's no *need* to, especially with Em as sick as she is; yes, I'll keep you posted." But he hadn't told Barney about the man, then, and he knew there would be no time for rest in the dormitory. No time for anything now but to find that man, whoever he was, wherever he was, somehow.

The first step was to scour the campus, building by building, class by class, professor by professor. For a while he pretended to continue classes, but there wasn't time for classes. Nothing turned up the first week, or the next, until the silly secretary in the registrar's office took his sudden attentions for real and got him a key to the faculty files, complete with mug shots, and he found who the man was at last. Name: Paul Conroe, psychology research associate; specialist in statistical analysis and probability theory; taught one class a week; B.S. from Princeton, Master's from Yale, a one-year research grant here. But when Jeff went after him, the man was gone. Everybody was puzzled; one morning the man had just failed to turn up at the lab in the psych building and nobody knew where he'd gone. *What* morning? The morning after Jeff had tried to chase him. No record of where he went, but there was a permanent mailing address, somewhere halfway across the country.

Jeff Meyer had gone back to his room then and written a very plausible letter to the dean explaining that a pressing family crisis made his temporary withdrawal from classes necessary, effective that day (after all, Em *had* been down with one of those vicious new viruses, and Barney had sounded worried on the phone), and that night Jeff was on the nonstop flight East. He didn't know where he was going, for sure, or what he was going to do. He knew just two things, both irrational and both true: first, that Paul Conroe had murdered his father; second, that it *mattered* to him, even though he could barely remember his father and knew nothing about his death. It mattered to him more than anything had ever mattered before. He didn't know why, but Paul Conroe had to be found. The long search had begun.

And now, as he stood in a volunteer's room far beneath ground level at the Hoffman Medical Center, with the tortured breathing of the man next door still in his ears, Jeff knew that somewhere here it had to end. He finished dressing, then opened the door to the corridor. The air seemed more fresh, like a soothing breeze after the stuffy air of the room. Jeff started for the escalator. It was almost two o'clock, and he hurried, anxious to reach the mess hall before it closed. He fought aside thoughts of the man in the next room, blocked off the bitter memories of the long hunt for Conroe and centered his mind once again on the girl. The escalator creaked as he started down. If only he could check with Barney now, to make certain that the trail had really ended at the Hoffman Center, make sure that Conroe wasn't still somewhere outside, still running. One thing seemed certain: if he *were* here, he too would be faced with the testing and classification; he would be on the same grim road as Jeff himself. And as a newcomer, he too would be under suspcion and scrutiny.

Jeff stopped short on a landing, suddenly aware that he had lost count of the flights he had gone down. Too many, it must have been more than four. He moved around to the up staircase and stepped on. The escalator groaned, as if every moment would be its last, and Jeff stared dreamily at the moving wall, waiting, then passed the open well to the opposite side. . . .

. . . and stared at the pale, frightened face of the man on the down-going stairway. In the brief seconds while they passed, Jeff stood paralyzed; then with a cry he turned, half stumbling, half falling down the up-going stairs until he reached the opening, long seconds later, and vaulted across the barrier, crashing his shoulder against the wall as he went through. He caught a glimpse of the man running from the bottom of the stairs into a corridor, and he shouted again in a burst of rage. He took the steps three at a time, his mind numb to the pain as his foot struck the solid floor and twisted, sending him sprawling on one knee. Then he was on his feet again, running down the corridor.

It divided into two, going off in a Y. Both sides were dark, and both were empty. Jeff stood panting, staring helplessly. He started down one corridor, jerked open a door, looked into a small, empty office. He tried another door, and another. Then he turned and ran back to the Y, spun around the corner and ran pell-mell down the second corridor. Only his own desperate footfalls echoed back to him in the darkness.

Back at the Y, he sank down, still panting, sobbing aloud in his rage, clenching his fists as he tried to regain control. Rage was there, and frustration, but there was something else, too: a surge of wild elation. Because there wasn't any question any more. Paul Conroe was among the Mercy Men.

Two figures were approaching from the lighted corridor. One of them held a stun-gun trained on Jeff's chest; the other, a huge, powerful man, reached down and hauled him up by the collar. "What's your unit, Jack?"

Jeff saw the gray cloth of the man's jacket, the black cartridge belt over his shoulder. "17-D," he panted.

The blow caught him full on the chin, twisting his head around with a jolt. "Another wise guy, wandering around without a pass," the voice growled. "You scum really think you run this place, don't you?" The heel of a hand hit his jaw, and a fist caught him hard in the pit of the stomach. As he doubled over he saw a raised hand descending; something exploded behind his ear, and his knees buckled.

Later, vaguely, he was aware of the guards half carrying, half dragging him up an escalator, along a corridor. He heard the door open, and fell face down on the floor. The guard's voice said, "Here's your roommate, doll. Try to keep him home from now on," and the door slammed behind him.

Painfully Jeff raised himself on his hands, shook his head dazedly. He tried to stand up, and collapsed again.

"You having some trouble or something?" The voice from across the room was hard and insolent.

Jeff jerked his head up, painfully, staring. The girl blinked at him indifferently and pulled a frayed cigarette from her blue cotton shirt. She snapped a match with her thumb and touched off the smoke. Then she looked back at Jeff. "Sorry, Jack," said the girl called Blackie, "but it looks like we're going to be roomies. So you might as well get used to the idea."

## VII

IN THAT moment, Jeff Meyer did something he had very seldom done before: he lost all control of himself.

It had happened before. There was once, back when he had first gone to live with Barney and Em as a ten-year-old when he had gone for Barney, arms and legs flailing, consumed with mindless rage. He couldn't remember *why*, now; something to do with the blind spot in his memory after his father's death, no doubt. (No penetrating *that* wall; he'd tried, and it was rock solid.) It happened again the day he first saw Conroe three years ago . . . he might have killed anyone who had blocked his way, that day, before his energy was spent.

But this was different. Before, something that he didn't understand inside his mind had seemed to drive him. This time he knew exactly what was in his mind. He had seen this girl's face on Dr. Schiml's visiphone screen. And he had seen it the night before in the tavern, the singer with long raven hair who had promised to deliver Conroe to him, and then sold him out. Now something exploded in his mind; he lurched across the room at the girl, catching her by the shoulders so hard the cigarette went flying. "All right," he grated, "where is he? Come on, come on, *talk.* I know he's in here, don't tell me he isn't. I just saw him down below. I just *chased* him. *Now where has he gone to?*"

The girl wrenched away, kicking him in the shin and trying to dodge past him. When he reached out to stop her she caught his arm, twisting it with amazing agility, and sent him reeling back against the wall. He hit hard; by the time his head cleared she was halfway across the room, facing him in a half-crouch with a knife held low in her right hand, blade up. Her eyes were wide in anger, and her lips twisted. "Don't take a step, buddy," she warned. "Not a step."

Jeff stared at her, and felt his heart sink. He hardly noticed the knife, it was her *face* that bothered him, now that he saw it more clearly. Something was wrong, somehow. The lips were not right, the nose was a little too long, the cheek bones a little too high. The resemblance was surely there, at first glance, but looking closer, there was too much wrong. She was not the girl in the nightclub at all. He spread his hands helplessly. "Where—where is he?" he asked.

"Where is who?"

"Conroe . . ." Jeff said, his voice trailing off. He shook his head, trying to clear it, trying to understand. This was surely the girl he had seen on the visiphone screen, yes—the same face, the same clothes. But she wasn't the girl in the nightclub. "Conroe," he repeated plaintively. "You know, Conroe?"

"I've never heard of Conroe."

"But you *must* have—last night, in that club, singing—"

She stared at him for a moment. Then she snapped the knife blade closed and sank down on her bed, her face relaxing into disgust. "Go away," she said tiredly. "That lousy Frenchman's sense of humor—I might have expected it." She looked up at him. "Go on, beat it," she repeated. "I'm not rooming with any crazy hophead, Frenchman or no Frenchman. Go find somebody else to bug. Not me."

"You don't even *know* Conroe?"

The girl looked at him closely. "Look, Jack," she said, "I don't know who you are, and I don't know your pal Conroe either. And I sure wasn't in any club last night singing. I was down in the tank last night helping Dr. Barnes get a crazy man cooled off enough for them to operate on his head this morning, and it wasn't fun for any of us, and believe me, you'll be down in the tank yourself pretty soon if you don't quit jumping people for no reason. And you won't like it there, either. Now go away, quit bothering me."

Jeff sank down on the opposite bed, his head in his hands. "You look so much like her."

"So I look so much like her," she mocked. "Just wait 'til I get my hands on that Frenchman." She pulled her legs up under her, glaring at him.

"All right, I'm sorry," Jeff said. "So I got excited. I couldn't help it. As for me going anywhere, you're out of luck. Last time I took a walk in this place I ran into a couple of fists."

Blackie laughed. "Of course you did. The guards don't like us a bit. They'll knock you around every time you give them a chance."

"But why? I wasn't doing anything."

The girl laughed harshly. "Nothing but wandering around where you didn't belong. You greenhorns do it every time. You might as well face it, Jack, you're in prison. They don't call it that, and there aren't any bars,

49

but you're not going *anywhere*, and the boys in gray are here to see that you don't. They hate us because we're in line for the kind of money they don't even dare try for. They've got to make out on a guard's salary, while we're gambling for big money even if it means getting our brains jarred loose. I mean that's what we're doing here, isn't it?" She looked up at him, her eyes narrowing. "Or is it?"

"I suppose so," Jeff said. "That's why I'm here. I'm waiting for testing. This other thing, about Conroe, that's just an old private fight. You wouldn't understand. You just look so much like the girl—" He studied her face more closely. She wasn't as young as he had thought at first; there were little wrinkles around her eyes, a little too much makeup showing. Her lips were painted too full, and there was a tiredness in her eyes, a beaten look that she couldn't quite hide. She leaned back on the bed, but even relaxing didn't erase the hardness in her face. Only the jet black hair and the smooth black eyebrows looked young and fresh. Jeff shook his head. "But I still don't get what you're doing here."

"This is my room," she said. "I live here."

"But I was assigned here."

"Yeah. That lousy Frenchman's sense of humor. I always get the greenhorns."

Jeff looked at her. "Well, are you one of the workers?"

"You mean one of the experimental animals?" she sneered. "Sure. One of the Mercy Men. Full of mercy, that's me." Suddenly she laughed. "What did you think, they'd have a separate boudoir for the ladies? Come off it, Jack! How do they treat any kind of experimental animal? They don't care what we do or how we live. All they want is good healthy human livestock when their experiments call for it. Nothing more. That means they have to feed us and bunk us down. Period. So I'm stuck, as usual. But if you've got any wise ideas, just try something. Just once. You'll find out I don't like looneys for roommates."

Jeff leaned back on his bunk, his hands trembling. The room seemed fuzzy as he watched it, and he felt his muscles sagging in pain and fatigue. He had counted so much on information from the girl when he saw her face on the visiphone screen, but obviously she wasn't the girl in the nightclub. A superficial resemblance, nothing else. Now, suddenly, he felt dreadfully alone, whipped, helpless to go on. Where could he go? How could he keep on a trail that always led into stone walls? He stretched out, yielding to his fatigue, and a sense of hopelessness. Maybe, he thought wearily, Barney was right, and he would never find Conroe. He sighed as the darkness of utter exhaustion closed in on him, and sank his head back on the pillow.

*Maybe the nightmares would never stop.*

## VIII

HE KNEW he was dreaming. Some tiny corner of his mind kept prodding him, telling him he dare not sleep, he should be up and moving, hunting; there was no time for sleep, but still he slept, uneasily, and dreamed. . . .

He was walking beside a brook, a walk he had taken before, many years ago. A breeze came from the meadow, rumpling his hair, and he could hear the water gurgle as it swirled across the rocks. A pleasant spot on a summer afternoon, but something about it frightened him, held him back at every footstep. Something in his mind was warning him, urging him away. *Get away, Jeff. Stop while you can. If you go any farther you'll be dead.*

He tried to ignore the warning and go on, but his legs wouldn't move. Suddenly, in this sunny place, a wave of fear swept over him and he turned and ran like the wind. And as he ran, it was the time he had been here before. He was no longer a man but a little boy running, crying out in fear. Then a man loomed up with arms outstretched and Jeff threw himself into his father's arms, sobbing as though his heart would break, clutching at him with incredible relief, burying his face in the strong, comforting chest. *Oh, daddy, youre here, you're safe. . . .*

He looked up at his father's smiling face, saw the strong, sensitive lines around his mouth, the power and wisdom in his eyes. Nowhere else in the world did he feel this sense of strength, of unlimited power, of complete comfort. He hugged Jacob Meyer fiercely, feeling a deep peacefulness flood his mind.

Then, abruptly something changed and he was afraid again, more frightened than ever before. He looked up and screamed because it wasn't his father holding him but another man, a man with a high forehead and prominent eyes and a thin bloodless face . . . *Conroe's face.* He screamed again, trying to struggle away, but Conroe held him as his terror grew. *He killed your father, Jeff. He murdered your father, shot him down like an animal, in cold blood.*

But *why? Why* did he do it? There was no answer. Suddenly Conroe was gone, no longer holding him. The meadow and the brook were gone, and Conroe was fleeing, a tiny distant figure running like the wind down a narrow, darkened hospital corridor. And Jeff was trying vainly to catch up with the fleeing figure. The walls were of gray stone; Conroe was running free, but Jeff could make no progress at all. Gray-clad guards appeared from the walls to block him. Dodging them, he tripped and fell, scrambled up again as the figure disappeared around a far corner. He reached the Y and found both corridors empty. When he glimpsed the running figure next it was far ahead, but they were no longer in the Hoffman Center. They were running down a hillside, a brown, barren hillside, studded with long knives and spears and swords, their shiny blades standing straight up from the ground, gleaming in the brazen light. Conroe was far ahead, moving nimbly through the gauntlet of swords, but Jeff couldn't follow any more. He stood panting as the figure vanished in the distance, and then he sank down to the ground, weeping, his whole body shaking in desperate, helpless sobs. And in his ears the voice of the girl, mocking him: *You'll never get him, Jeff, no matter how hard you try. Never, never, never.*

"But I've got to," he cried out. *"Daddy told me to. . . ."*

He woke with a jolt, his voice still echoing in the room. He sat bolt upright, looking for his watch, not finding it—*how long had he slept?* Across the room the opposite bed was empty. He groaned, rolling to his feet with the horrible feeling that he had missed something while he slept. Something critically important. Again he looked for his watch—it was no longer on his wrist.

With a curse he crossed the room and threw open Blackie's foot locker. Sure enough, the watch lay there, on top of the heap of gold jewelry nested in the dirty clothes. He stared at it as he restrapped it on his wrist. Then he walked into the lavatory, splashed cold water into his face, trying to quiet the painful throbbing in his head. The watch said 8:30 P.M.

He had lost five precious hours. Five hours for Conroe to hide, cover his tracks, disappear still deeper into this pile of human rubble. Jeff stumbled to the door, opened it a crack, then closed it as two gray-clothed guards passed by in the corridor. Violently hungry, he searched the room. Finally he found some crackers and a chunk of cheese at the bottom of Blackie's locker. He devoured them, washing them down with water from the lavatory tap. Then he sank down on the edge of the bed.

The dream again, the same nightmare as always. He had dreamed it many times before, long before he had ever seen Conroe. Always different details, but the same dream. The face that had haunted him for as long as he could remember, the face that had almost driven him out of his mind the day he met it on the library steps three years ago. The face of the man he had hunted ever since but never caught, a man who had dodged every trap with relentless agility, but finally had become so desperate to escape him that he had fled into this nightmare hospital world to avoid confrontation.

Jeff shook his head, hopelessly trying to find some sense to it. This was a half-world of avaricious men and women, selling themselves for incredible fees, a half-world even more insane than the warped world of pressure and creeping madness that lay outside the Hoffman Center. And in this half-world were a doctor who knew that Jeff was a fraud, a kleptomaniac girl who thought he was an addict, and somewhere, the slender figure of the man he hunted, still running.

This time when he looked out the guards were gone. Somewhere to his right he heard a burst of laughter and the sound of many voices. The smell of coffee floated down the hall to tantalize him. He followed the sounds, turned a corner, and found himself at the door of a long, large room serving as recreation hall and lounge for the Mercy Men in his unit.

The room was crowded with people. A dozen groups were standing together, sitting at gaming tables or huddled on the floor in a buzz of frantic excitement. In the hard white glare of the wall lights he saw dice rolling in the center of some groups. He heard the riffle of playing cards and the harsh, tense laugh of a winner claiming his pot. And then the Nasty Frenchman was there beside him, his eyes bright with excitement, a cup of exceedingly black coffee in one hand and a pile of white paper tags in the other. He grinned at Jeff with undisguised malice.

"It's about time you turned up," he said, "we were about to go get you. With all that money coming up, you wouldn't want to miss a chance to make a few bets, would you? Come on in, wise guy, things are just getting hot."

Blinking, Jeff Meyer walked into the room.

## Part Two

## THE QUARRY

### I

THE MOMENT he stepped into the crowded room, Jeff's impulse was to turn and run. There was no explaining the sudden wave of panic that surged up in him, no rationalizing the overpowering sense of dread and danger that he felt. But the feeling was there: a feeling of unbearable *wrongness* in this room.

He walked in slowly, felt the door tug his hand as he closed it, as though a draft of air in the corridor was sucking it shut behind him. Except for the Nasty Frenchman, nobody seemed to notice him. Everyone was fiercely intent on the rolling dice or the cards being dealt. Jacques motioned him to follow and began shouldering through the crowd. Jeff followed, watching in amazement.

It was a gaming room, and the tables were obviously hot. From an overhead speaker one of Silly Giggin's shock-beat jazz arrangements was pounding insistently, but the room was filled with a rattle of tense voices, even over the music. Most of the faces were new to Jeff—tired, worn-out faces, marked with fear, hunted faces stamped with resignation and hopelessness. He saw compressed, bloodless lips, eyes that were cold and cynical, often very sharp, intelligent faces, but twisted somehow. Crowds leaned tensely around the players at the tables, watching the cards closely, laying side bets as the hands were opened. Other groups huddled on the floor, momentarily hushed as the dice were rolled. The music pounded and scraped; little bursts of laughter broke out to compete with it. And for Jeff, a growing sense of something twisted and distorted here, of something gone horribly wrong. . . .

He searched the room as he moved among the players. Far across the room he saw Blackie. Their eyes met for a moment, and his feeling of something gone wrong intensified. He stopped at a dice huddle, tapped a man on the shoulder. "How do you get in?" he asked, pointing to the game.

The man looked at him strangely. "You put down your money and you play," he said. "How else? If you're broke, there's always your next big payoff to borrow on. What's wrong, you new around here or something?" The man moved on, shaking his head.

Suddenly it made sense—at least part of it did. What would be more plausible than high-stake gambling in a world where the people were teetering on the brink of death from day to day? They were gambling their very lives here; of course they would be gambling their money as well. The need for excitement, for violent tension release, must be overpowering in this dismal prisonlike place. And with fortunes yet unearned to bet with—! Jeff shivered. Cutthroat games, too, but the Hoffman Center people wouldn't interfere. They would probably even encourage it—what better way to keep a stable crew of Mercy Men on hand than to let them indenture themselves to their own money lenders. This, at least, made sense; but it didn't really explain the pervading, explosive tension that had seemed to charge the atmosphere the moment he had walked in.

He watched the dice game for a while, then crossed the room to find the Nasty Frenchman again. The little man was gulping black coffee in the corner, talking intently to a bald-headed giant who leaned against the wall, facing him. Jeff spotted Blackie, huddled across the room on her knees, facing a buck-toothed man as she rolled three colored dice in swift repetitive movements, again and again. With each roll her eyes followed the dice, quick, unnaturally bright. Jeff shook his head. Of all dice games, Hanoi was the roughest, a high-speed, high-tension game for people with steel nerves. Most legal casinos banned it; the famous deadlocks of the game too often led to murder as the pots rose higher and higher.

The girl seemed to be winning, now; she rolled the dice with trancelike regularity, and the buck-toothed man turned gray as his money pile dwindled. Across the room a crap game was moving swiftly, with staggering sums of money passing from hand to hand, and the card games, though slower, left the mark of their prolonged tension on the players' faces. Jeff kept looking until he had seen every face in the room.

Conroe was not here. He hadn't expected to find him, but then he hadn't expected to find this maddening sense of tension either. *What was happening here?* No one else seemed to notice anything. Could he be the only one who could feel the uncanny change in the air, in the sounds around him, even in the color of the light from the walls? Something impelled him to run, to get away, leave this room now, while he could. Yet when he tried to analyze what was bothering him, it kept wriggling out of his grasp.

Finally he reached the corner of the room. He heard the Nasty Frenchman's nasal voice talking to the bald-headed giant, and he paused, listening.

"I tell you, Harpo, I heard it with my own ears. You never saw Schiml so excited! And then, Louie Grekko was saying that their whole unit is being split up—that's the 19-C unit. I saw him when I was going through this afternoon. He was all stirred up too."

"But why a split-up?" The man called Harpo growled. "I wouldn't trust Louie's word for nothin', and as for you, I think you hear what you want to hear. What's the point of splitting up a unit? Schiml's coming along fine with the work he's using us for."

"That's just it," the Nasty Frenchman retorted. "We've been doing fine, and now something's going on that could put us right out in the cold. Can't you get that straight? Something's about to break. They're onto something big, Schiml and his boys, and they've got a new man, somebody they're really excited about; somebody who can knock down walls just by looking at them, and things like that."

Harpo made a disgusted noise. "You mean the old ESP story again," he said. "So why get so worried? Look, all you've got to do is whisper 'extra-sensory perception' to Schiml and you automatically send him off on another spook hunt. You know that. But that's all it is: a spook hunt. That's all it ever was. Pretty soon Schiml will get over it, same as he did the last time, and the time before, and things will go back to normal again."

"Maybe so . . . but this time they're changing things, and changes mean trouble." The Nasty Frenchman's voice was tense. He noticed Jeff, but went on. "Look, they start on a big program, a nice long term, low-risk program, and they assign us all jobs that carry good odds, they get the work all lined up for months in advance. And then all of a sudden something new comes along; they get excited about something. So what happens? They scratch *our* program, put us on ice maybe for months, scramble things up, change the fees, change the work, and then end up handing the big money to some greenhorn who just walked into the place. Well, I don't like it. I've been around too long. I've had too many tough, lousy jobs here for them to just shove me aside because they don't happen to be interested any more in what we were doing before. And they *never tell us*, either. We never know for sure, we just have to wait, and guess, and hope." The little man's eyes blazed. "Well, maybe they don't tell us, but I've got a little ESP myself. And I say this is no spook hunt this time. Something's wrong. Something's going to happen. I can feel it in the air in here right now."

Jeff Meyer's skin crawled. That was the answer, of course. That was why he couldn't pin down his violent uneasiness. Something was wrong, all right—*but it hadn't happened yet.* It was something that was *about* to happen! He stared at a group crouching around a Hanoi game, watched the brightly colored dice roll across and back, across and back. A newcomer, the Nasty Frenchman had said, someone who had come in and disrupted the smooth work schedule of the Center, someone who had gotten the doctors suddenly excited. And now they were planning a spook hunt. . . .

*What kind of a spook hunt?* Why that particular choice of word? Could Conroe conceivably be the newcomer Jacques was talking about? It seemed awfully soon for that; they'd have had to have tested him pretty quickly. But if not Conroe, who else? And what did this have to do with the insistent air of impending danger that pervaded the room, right now?

His eyes were still on the dice game, and then something suddenly came into focus. He wanted violently, irrationally, *not to look at those dice.* He frowned, angry with himself. Why not look? What was there so threatening about a dice game? He moved closer, watching the dice in fascination. Then he dropped to his knees to join the huddle.

"You in, buddy?" somebody asked. Jeff nodded. His mouth was dry as he pulled money from his pocket, placed the bills on the floor. Somebody handed him the dice. . . .

He faced the man with beady black eyes, and then raised the three colored dice, rolling them in the familiar pattern. The two of them deadlocked in four rolls, tying up the pot; then they sweated out seven more without a raise, neither of them daring to gamble on breaking it. Then Jeff felt a break in the odds, boosted the ante on his next throw, and held his breath as the man facing him matched it. The dice rolled and fell into deadlock again; around them people gasped, moved in closer to watch. A third set of dice went into play to try to break the deadlock, and then a fourth set as the complex structure of the game built up like a house of cards and the stakes multiplied. At last, Jeff's dice turned up the critical number and the deadlock began to fall apart, throw after throw, and the money moved into his hands. Four or five others moved in with side bets, collecting along with him, as he moved into another game, built it up, lost it cold, and still played on, his excitement growing.

Suddenly, a cry broke out in the room. Eyes glanced up, startled, at two men in a far corner who stood glaring at each other.

"Throw them down! Go on, *throw them down, see how they land!*"

Somebody shouted, "What happened, Archie?"

"He's got loaded dice!" Archie pointed an accusing finger at the other man. "They aren't falling right, there's something wrong with them!"

His opponent snarled. "So you aren't winning any more. So what? You brought those dice in yourself."

"But the odds aren't right. Something funny's going on."

Jeff turned back to his own game, sensing disaster hanging in the air. The game moved on, faster and faster. Somewhere across the room another fight broke out, and another. Several men dropped out of games, standing up against walls, their eyes wide with anger as they watched the other players. And then Jeff rolled three sixes fourteen times end-running, .and tossed the dice down in front of his gaping opponent without even picking up his heap of money, and walked shakily back to the corner, the whole room spinning around him.

*Because, suddenly, in this room, probabilities had gone mad.* He could feel the shifting tension of the atmosphere, as real and oppressive as if it were something solid he had to wade through. This was what had been bothering him, plaguing him all evening. Something impossible had begun to happen, suddenly, without explanation. Cards had begun to turn up in impossible sequences, repeating themselves with idiotic regularity. In every game the dice were falling wrong, defying the laws of gravity as they spun on the tables and floors. The room was in an uproar as the players stopped, and stared at each other, unable to comprehend the impossible that was happening before their eyes. *And Jeff had known it was going to happen all along!*

He saw Blackie move by, her face flushed, a curious light of desperation in her eyes. On impulse he reached and stopped her. "Game," he said sharply.

Her eyes flashed at him. "What game?"

"Any game." He held up his wrist watch. "We can play for this."

Something flared in her eyes for a moment. Then she was down on her knees with the dice, pushing her sleeves up, a tight look of fear in her eyes as she looked up at him. "Something's happening," she said softly. "The dice aren't right."

"I know it," he said. "Why not?"

She looked at him, a baffled look. "I don't know, there isn't any reason, but they don't fall right, they just don't."

Jeff grinned at her. "Go ahead, throw them."

She rolled the dice, saw them dance on the floor, called out her number. Jeff rolled them, beat her on it, picked up the money. He rolled again, then again. The tightness grew around the girl's eyes; little tense lines hardened near her mouth. Nervously she fumbled a cigarette into her mouth and lit it as the dice rolled.

She lost. She lost again. Side bets picked up around them, as the people watching caught the growing tension.

"What's happening?"

"The dice—they've gone crazy!"

"Blackie's losing, of all things!"

"*Losing?* She *never* loses with dice—who's the guy?"

"Never saw him before. Look, he took another one! Those dice are hexed."

"My cards were crazy, too. A straight flush every hand, six hands in a row. Now how can you bet on something like that?"

The shock-beat record screamed louder; then the speaker gave a squawk as somebody smashed in the record player with his foot. A pack of cards was hurled to the floor, and a scream broke out across the room. Two men came suddenly to blows over one dice game; several others hunched down to tight-lipped intensity between individuals. A huge man burst into tears, staring at his dice. "They can't act like this," he wailed, "they just *can't!*"

Jeff watched the spinning dice, rolling them, rolling them, and saw the girl's face darken with every throw. Suddenly she snatched them out of his hand in mid-throw and hurled them across the room, glaring at him and the onlookers like a cornered animal. "It's all of you," she snarled. "You're turning them against me, you're making them fall wrong." She turned and started for the door, still glowering at the people around her, but Jeff saw fear in her eyes too. He started after her, felt a restraining hand on his arm. "Leave her alone," said the Nasty Frenchman. "You'll be in trouble if you don't. You see what I meant about something being wrong? The whole crowd here is on edge. Who ever saw dice act that way, or cards fall like that? Unless *somebody had control of them.*"

Jeff stared at the man. "Control of all the dice in this room at once? What are you talking about?"

The little man's lips twisted angrily. "Well, what else? You see what's happening, don't you?"

Jeff turned away, shouldered his way through the

crowd to the door. The Nasty Frenchman had a point, maybe a part of the truth, but there was far more to it than that. It wasn't just somebody controlling dice. Suddenly Jeff knew that this hour just past in the game room held the key to everything, if only he could use it: the answer to the whole tangled puzzle of the girl and Paul Conroe, of Dr. Schiml and the Mercy Men.

The answer was here, he *knew* it was here with absolute certainty. He also knew that when he reached his room Blackie would be waiting for him, waiting with cold fire in her eyes, seated at the table, a set of colored dice before her in the dim light. Jeff hurried down the darkened corridor, fearful of what he knew. She would be there, and he knew *why* she would be there, smoldering, when he walked into the room. He had seen her eyes, and her face as they had thrown the dice, and he knew beyond any shadow of doubt who had been controlling the dice.

She was waiting, of course. He stepped into the room, closed and locked the door behind him. Then he met her desperate eyes as she rolled the colored dice back and forth in front of her.

"Game!" she challenged hoarsely.

Trembling, he sank down opposite her at the table.


## II


JEFF REACHED out and took the dice from the girl's hand. "Put them away, Blackie," he said softly. "You don't have to prove anything to me. I already know."

"Game," she repeated, shaking her head.

"No, think a minute. Back in the game room . . . *do you know what was happening in there?*"

Her eyes caught his, wide with fear. "Game," she

whispered, her hands trembling. *"You've got to play me!"*

He sighed, suddenly very tired, and rolled the dice out on the table. A three, a four, and a five fell; she nodded, taking in the sequence. Then she reached, took the dice, gave them a throw. He could feel her anger, and he gripped the table edge as the dice danced, and settled down: a three, a four, and a five.

The girl stared at him, then back at the dice. Slowly she reached out for the one with the five showing, sent it rolling across the table. It spun, and bounced, and settled down once again with the five exposed. With a trembling hand she picked up all three, threw them out hard, clenched her fists as they fell. The three and four settled out immediately. Jeff watched the third cube, spinning on one corner, spinning and spinning— he felt his chest tighten as he stared at the little cube, as though something were squeezing the breath out of him—and the little cube continued, ridiculously, to spin and spin, until it flipped over abruptly on its side, and lay still.

With the five exposed.

Blackie cried out, her face chalky white. "Then it was you!" she said. *"You* were doing it in there, doing it deliberately, twisting the odds around, turning the dice against me."

"No," Jeff shook his head violently. "Not me—*us.* Both of us together. Neither of us could have made *that* happen alone, but we were really fighting each other, without knowing it, and that was when it started happening."

"Don't try to tell me that," she retorted. "It was *you!*"

In answer, Jeff pointed to the dice on the table. Blackie stared at them in horror as the one with the five up twitched, like a jumping bean, twitched again, rolled over, began turning and spinning on one corner in an incredible grotesque little dance. "I want a five," he said. "You make it turn up any other number you think you can. Go ahead, do your damnedest!" And the cube continued to spin crazily on its corner, refusing to fall at all. . . .

Finally she hit it with her hand, knocked it across the room.

"Couldn't do it, hm?"

"You knew all along," she accused him. "You came in there just to torment me tonight, just to show me up."

"That's just it," Jeff said. "I *didn't* know, until I picked up the dice in that room. All I knew was that something was going to happen, I didn't know what. Even then I didn't realize what it was, except that the dice were doing what I wanted them to do while your game was going sour." His eyes sought the girl's. "You've got to believe me: I had no idea it was you. But I knew somebody was fighting me, somebody was tampering with the dice. Somebody who *always* had tampered with the dice before and got away with it, and now all of a sudden couldn't make them behave any more."

The girl's face was working, tears welling up in her eyes. "I had to—I had to win with them—"

"And then when *both* of us started tampering with them, fighting each other, the probabilities governing the games started to go wild, completely wild."

The girl was sobbing now, her face buried in her hands. "I could always control them, I could always make it work, it was the only thing I *could* do that ever came out right. Everything else always went wrong, always." She wept like a baby, her shoulders shaking.

Jeff leaned forward, touched her hair. "When did you find out you could make dice fall the way you wanted them to?"

The girl shook her head helplessly. "I didn't know it until I came to this place. I never knew it before. And then, when I found out, it was the *only* thing I could win at. I lost at everything else. All my life I've been losing."

"*What* have you been losing?"

"Everything. Everything I touch turns black, goes sour, somehow. Everything always has."

"But *what* has?" Jeff stared at her. "What are you doing here? Why did you come here in the first place?"

"I don't know," she said in a beaten tone. "What else was there to do? Oh, I was a tough kid, believe me. I could take it up to a point, but it kept getting worse and worse until I couldn't stand it any more. Everything I tried went wrong, and it hit everybody near me as well." She looked up at him defiantly, brushed her hair back from her eyes. "Look, I may not be a knockout to look at, but I'm not so repulsive either, am I? Well, why do you think I didn't have a roomie when they brought you in here? Because nobody wants to be that near me, that's why! I get the greenhorns every time until they start breaking legs or something, and then they get wise and find some other place to go, *any* place!" She sniffled. "On the outside, it got so bad even the rackets wouldn't work right when I was around."

"What rackets?"

"Any of the rackets, I've been in a dozen since the war. Dad was killed in the first bombing, when I was just a kid, twelve, thirteen, I can't remember now. He died trying to get us out of the city and through to the safety area up north. Radiation burns got him, maybe pneumonia, I don't know, but Dad went first, and later it got Mom too." She straightened up, wiping her eyes with her sleeve. "We never did get out of the devastated area—we were killing dogs and cats for a while. Then when it was all over there was the inflation, the burnt-out crops, the whole rat race. There were plenty of dirty breaks then; first we were guerrillas, then bushwhackers, then we came back to the city to shake down the rich ones that had been hiding in the mountains getting richer."

"But how did you end up *here*, if that was going so well?"

"It wasn't, that's just it. The luck was running wrong, worse and worse and worse all the time. Then I got hooked on dope for a while. Narcotics control was coming back fast, but there was stuff around, and everybody in the rackets knew I had this hard luck jinx and got me hooked solid." She shrugged. "Well, finally I came here and Schiml sold me his bill of goods. He promised to get me off the stuff. And what could I lose? I was too tired to care about anything, then, all I wanted was to eat, and get off the stuff, and get enough cash together to try something decent, maybe, something where hard luck couldn't touch me."

"And then you found out about the dice," Jeff said.

"And how. I found out I could make them sit up and talk for me. I took it easy, of course, I didn't let anybody catch on, sometimes I'd even deliberately lose so they wouldn't get suspicious, but they *always* worked for me. Until tonight."

Jeff nodded. "Until tonight, you found yourself fighting for control. Because tonight I found out they'd talk for me, too. And you couldn't beat me with them."

Her voice was weak. "I—I couldn't make them budge. They fell the way you called them."

"It isn't possible, you know," Jeff said softly. "Scientists have been trying to document it for centuries, and they've never succeeded. Nobody's ever proved that psychokinesis or other extrasensory powers even exist."

Blackie grinned without humor. "Schiml has been trying to prove it since the year one. Every now and again he gets hot on it again. Like right now, they must have just tested somebody who's got them all excited; they're setting up a whole new program."

"Yes," Jeff said, "and that's where I came in. Who is that somebody?"

"I don't know. I just heard rumors. A new recruit, I guess."

"A recruit named Conroe?"

She looked at him. "I don't know. I don't even know for sure there is somebody."

"Well, I've got to find out. And you can help me." Jeff's voice trembled. "I know he's here, I saw him this afternoon on the stairs. Remember when the guards brought me in here? I'd seen him, and chased him and he got away from me, and then the guards found me. But he's sure to be here, hiding somewhere.

"What do you want with him?" Blackie asked. "Why are you after him? I don't want to get mixed up in anything."

"No, you won't be involved at all. And I can't tell you the whole thing, it doesn't even make sense to me. But this man, this Conroe, killed my father. I don't know why or how, but I need to know. That's all."

She obviously didn't believe him, but she merely shrugged. "And you say that the man is here?"

"He's here, all right. I've got to find him, before I get in too deep. Before I'm tested and assigned. I need to move fast, and I need help. You could help."

For a long while the girl sat silent, staring at the table between them. At length she picked up the dice, turned them around in her hand. "I told you I've been playing it smart here, with the dice—until you turned up," she said softly. "I could go on playing it smart, too," She looked up at him. "If you let me."

"I see," he said slowly. "It looks as if I don't have much choice. But you'll have to produce. I need floor plans of this place and information on how to avoid the guards. I need to know where the records are kept, the personnel rosters, the program plans. . . ."

"Then it's a deal?" she said eagerly.

He caught her eyes. For an instant he saw something back of her eyes, something of the fear that lay there. He saw a flickering trace of a little child, fighting against impossible odds to find a toehold, fighting a battle she knew she was losing, appealing to him for help.

Then it was gone and her eyes were blank again, revealing nothing.

Jeff reached out, touched her hand, squeezed her fingers lightly. "It's a deal," he said.

## III

SOMEWHERE down the corridor ahead a light from a doorway went out. Jeff Meyer stopped, watching, then ducked into a janitor's alcove as footsteps approached. Backed into a pile of brooms and mops, he waited, holding his breath as someone went by, wearing the blue fatigue clothing of the Mercy Men.

Bound for the game room, probably, Jeff thought. Or somewhere. It didn't matter. He took a relieved breath and decided to wait where he was for a while longer before going on.

He and Blackie had talked for two hours, maybe three, he wasn't sure. She had been in the Center for over two years, and she was sharp; she knew what he wanted to know. It was too late for dinner in the cafeteria, and he was nearly famished; when he mentioned his hunger, the girl went into the lavatory and hauled out an amazing cache of canned food that he had missed, hidden in a linen closet. Also a purloined can opener, a plate and fork, and after some prolonged hesitation and soul-searching, a can of beer. He marveled; this girl obviously spent her spare time robbing people blind. She must have been working on the commissary for a long, long time.

"Well," she said defensively, "what else can you do? No candy or gum machines in the game room—might throw blood sugars off. And no alcohol, you can bet; if somebody comes in here that really needs it, they dry him out first."

He feasted. Then they went over floor plans and building organization. At last he was ready to leave, with at least a vague idea as to where he was going.

He had thought, when he started toward the escalator, that he had put the experience in the game room out of his mind for a moment. Now he found he was wrong. He was still reeling from the impossible discovery about the dice: the sudden, incredible awareness that he and Blackie had been silently and fiercely fighting each other for control, fighting with a fury that had somehow shattered the very warp of probablility in that crowded gaming room. But how could he have contributed to something like that? He had had no suspicion, not even a hint, that he might be carrying such an ability, yet here was evidence he could not disregard. And how did this relate to Paul Conroe, or to the mysterious recruit to the Mercy Men who had just been tested? Could Conroe be that man? No way to tell.

And yet. . . .

*Think about it, Jeff. Think of the long record of escapes, the multitude of times that Conroe eluded you when there was no apparent way that he could. Coincidence? Good luck? Maybe. But if Conroe had hidden extrasensory powers, he might keep on eluding you . . . unless you could find some way to oppose them.*

Jeff shook his head angrily. *How could he tell?* He had no evidence that Conroe had any extrasensory capabilities whatever; if he had, there was certainly no sign that he knew about them. There were so many, many possibilities, and so little concrete evidence to go on. If Conroe did have such capabilities, why had he been so startled to meet Jeff on the stairs? Why the look of fear and disbelief—almost panic—on his face? Jeff glanced at his watch, saw the minute hand move to 11:30. He couldn't wait any longer, he would have to hurry. The guards would be coming down the escalator in a few moments. And this kind of thinking led nowhere. Conroe *had* been shocked to see him. It must have given Conroe quite a jolt to realize that the hunter had followed him in here, to realize that he was going to have to take the risk of actual assignment to work as a Mercy Man.

But if he was shocked and frightend, what would he have done? Jeff had no idea.

A thousand ideas flooded his mind. He himself was waiting for testing; perhaps Conroe, somehow, had already been tested. Could he succeed in stalling Schiml, especially if the rumors he had heard in the game room were true? There was no way to be sure. All that Jeff could do was to search the file rooms Blackie had directed him to, try to find out where in this maze Conroe was and what he was doing. He stopped at the top of the escalator, studied Blackie's sketch of the floor plan again. The filing rooms were two flights below, if he could reach them without being stopped. He walked onto the down staircase, alert for guards.

At the bottom he stopped short. Three men in white were pushing a wheeled stretcher along the corridor. Jeff glanced at the twitching form under the blankets, then looked away hurriedly. One of the men dropped behind, calling him over as he stepped off the stairs. The man still wore the operating mask hanging from his neck, and his hair was tightly enclosed in the green knit operating cap. He tipped a thumb over his shoulder, pointing down the corridor. "You coming to fix the pump?"

Jeff blinked. "That's right," he croaked. "Did—did Jerry bring the tools yet?"

"Nobody's been here yet, we just finished. Been in there since three this afternoon, and the pump went out right in the middle of it. Had to aspirate the poor guy by hand, and if you think *that's* not a job—" The doctor wiped his forehead. "Better get it fixed tonight; we've got another one going in at eight in the morning, and we've got to have the pump—"

"Don't you worry, we'll fix it." Jeff started down the hall, his heart racing. He reached the open door to one of the operating rooms, slipped quickly into the small dressing-room annex, and snatched up one of the gowns and caps from the wall. If they were still operating this late, it was a heaven-sent chance; no guard would dare to bother him if he were wearing the white of a doctor, or the green of a surgeon. He struggled into the clumsy gown, tying it quickly behind his back, and slipped the cap over his head. Finally he found a surgical mask, snapped it on as he had seen it worn by the doctor in the corridor.

A moment later he was back on the escalator, descending to the next floor. At the foot of the stairs he started quickly down the passageway Blackie had indicated, glancing at each door as he passed. The first two had lights under them—apparently operating rooms still in use. Finally he stopped before a large, heavy door, with a sign painted on the wooden panel: AUTHORIZED PERSONNEL ONLY. He tried the door, found it locked. Quickly he dug in his pocket for the stolen key Blackie had produced after a certain amount of negotiation. It fit the lock, and he was inside.

No point tip-toeing around, he decided, with the surgeon's rig for a cover. Light showing under a closed door would excite more suspicion than a medically clad person out in the open apparently engaged in some legitimate record searching. He left the door wide open and snapped on the overhead lights, filling the room with a bright fluorescent glare. Then he drew the surgeon's gown tighter and crossed the room to the huge cross-index file console.

It wasn't the first time Jeff had encountered the kind of massive punched-card file which had become so necessary in organizations where the sheer volume of records to be kept made old-fashioned filing either too slow or too clumsy or both. As for hospitals and the like, the old kind of thick patient charts had gone out almost completely by the 1980's. Today modern file computers took dictated notes direct from the tape, matched terms and phrases with hundreds of thousands of programmed vocabulary-bits, analyzed them, identified them with code patterns, and punched the information onto cards, so that a patient's lifetime medical history could be permanently stored on a single small strip of plastic. When specific information was needed, the computer file reversed the process, extracted the requested data and fed it through read-out equipment that produced neat typescript on cheap, easily disposable paper. All the human operator needed was some notion of the classes of information that would be recorded, and that, Jeff thought, he could pretty well guess.

He moved quickly to the master control panel, searched for the input keyboard, and typed a request for coding under Research: Volunteer Personnel. First he would try the simple coding for Conroe's name, on the chance that Conroe might have given his own name when he came in, just as Jeff had done, for fear of being caught in a lie and thrown out the door. When the code card came down he punched the necessary buttons for an alphabetical scan for Conroe's name, and waited as the machinery whirred briefly. Presently a strip of read-out tape appeared, bearing two words: NO INFORMATION.

Jeff's fingers sped over the coding board again, as he started building a description. He coded in height, weight, eye color, hair color, bone contour, nose formation, every other descriptive category he could think of. Then he punched the File Search button. This time several dozen card copies appeared in the read-out tray. He picked them up and went through them slowly, glancing at the small photographs attached to each card, and at the date of admission code symbol on each.

Again he found nothing.

Disgusted, he tried the same system again, this time adding two limiting coding symbols: Volunteer Personnel and Recent Admission. Fewer cards. this time, but again all negative. Not a single one could possibly have been connected with Paul Conroe.

Jeff sat down at the desk facing the panel, searching his mind for some other avenue to identification. A thought struck him. Hospital file computers were pretty sophisticated, and the Hoffman Center would have the most efficient and flexible system possible. He dug out his wallet and extracted a small ID photo of Conroe he had carried for identification purposes. After a search, he found the small photo-scanning chamber used to record or scan photographs. He slipped the photo into the chamber, punched both the Scan and the Search buttons, and waited again.

This took longer, but after a few moments a single card dropped into the slot. Eagerly Jeff snatched it up, stared down at the photograph attached which almost perfectly matched the photo from his pocket. Near the top of the card was a brief notation, obviously hand-typed: Conroe, Paul A., Information Restricted. All File Notations Recorded in Hoffman Center Central Archives. Authorization Required.

Below this notation, a list of dates were typed in. Jeff stared at them in disbelief. Incredible, those dates, over two dozen of them: dates of admission to the Hoffman Center; dates of release; dates of outpatient follow-up visits. It was impossible that Conroe could have been here at the times the dates indicated—ten years ago, when the Hoffman Center was hardly opened, again five years ago, then more frequent admissions recently during the very time Jeff had been trailing him. It just didn't make sense that Conroe could have been here all those different times without Jeff having known it; but the dates were there on the card in black and white; cold, impersonal, indisputable. And following the last date, a final notation, inked in by hand: *Central Archives Classification: ESP Research.*

It was incredible, but it meant *something.* Quickly

Jeff stuffed the card into his shirt, tossing the unwanted card copies into the disposal chute. Whatever it meant, it fit into the picture. Next step would have to be the General Archives. He turned, started for the door, and then stopped dead in his tracks.

"Well, good evening," a man said from the door.

"Schiml!" Jeff exclaimed.

The doctor was leaning against the door jamb, green cap askew on his head, mask still dangling about his neck. He smiled at Jeff as he nonchalantly tossed a pair of dice into the air and caught them again. "I didn't want to interrupt anything," he said, "but we've been looking all over for you. We've got some tests to run."

"You—you mean in the morning," Jeff stammered.

Dr. Schiml's smile broadened and he shook his head. He tossed the dice again, then dropped them in his pocket. "Not in the morning, Jeff," he said softly. "Now."

## IV

JEFF SAT back, staring at the man in the doorway and trying to regain control of his trembling muscles. How long had Dr. Schiml been standing there? For just a few seconds? Or for ten minutes or more, watching Jeff punch out filing code numbers, watching him stuff the card copy into his shirt? He could tell nothing from the doctor's smiling face, nor from the guards who stood behind him in the corridor, hands poised on the holstered stun-guns. Schiml nodded to them and they disappeared, their boots clacking down the hall. Then the doctor turned back to Jeff, a ghost of a smile still flickering in his eyes. "Find anything interesting?" he asked.

"Not much," Jeff said hoarsely. "It's been a long time

since I worked one of those files." His eyes caught Schiml's eyes defiantly, and held them. After a moment Schiml shrugged. He walked to the file console, checked the read-out box for cards.

"Was there some special thing you were looking for?" he asked.

"Nothing special."

"I see. Just sort of sightseeing, I suppose."

Jeff shrugged. "More or less. I wanted to see the setup."

Schiml chuckled. "Particularly the medical records setup," he said. "Well, I guess it figures. Blackie insisted you'd gone to the game room when we came for you, but you weren't there. Oddly enough, this was the first place I thought to start looking." The doctor's eyes hardened. "All dressed up like a doctor, too—" He reached out and jerked the cap from Jeff's head, snapped the string to the gown with a sharp tug. "Get something straight: you don't wear these clothes in this place, *ever*. Doctors wear these clothes, nobody else. Is that clear? Fine. You also do not wander around breaking into filing rooms, just looking at the setup. If the guards had caught you at it, you wouldn't be alive right now, which would have been quite a shame, since we have plans for you." He held out his hand. "The key, please. Blackie supplied it, no doubt. She must have a dozen of them hidden somewhere; every time we change a lock, she's got a key to it the next day." He took the key from Jeff, dropped it in the same pocket the dice had gone into. "Okay, let's go. We've got some work to do."

Jeff fell into stride with him in the corridor. "You aren't serious about testing me tonight?"

"I'm perfectly serious. Why not?"

"Well—it's late. I'll be here in the morning. What's the rush?"

The doctor walked on in silence, ignoring him. Jeff kept up with him, trying to sort out a dozen questions in his mind. How much did Schiml know? How much did he suspect? What was he doing with those dice? Had Blackie told him? No, that didn't add up: she wanted that kept quiet more than he did. But maybe Schiml had heard about the freakish occurrence in the game room through other channels. Maybe. As for the testing—this he *really* didn't like. "Look," he blurted, "unless there's some frantic reason that you have to run these tests at midnight, why can't we just wait until morning?"

Schiml stopped short and turned to Jeff in exasperation. "I'll be damned," he said. "You still think that we're running a picnic ground here, don't you? Some sort of charity ward. Well, we're not. We're doing a job, a job that can't wait for morning. Morning! We work a twenty-four-hour schedule; the work doesn't quit and go home for the night. And all you are expected to do is to provide the wherewithal for the work to go on, when and where it is needed. Nothing more."

"But I'll be tired, nervous—I don't see how I could hope to pass any kind of test now."

Schiml snorted. "That doesn't matter. These aren't the kinds of tests that you pass or fail. Matter of fact, the more tired and nervous you are, the better off you'll be. The tests will give you an extra margin of safety when job assignment comes around. The tests tell us what we can expect from you, the very minimum. Basically, we're working hard to try to save your life for you."

Frowning, Jeff followed him through swinging doors into a long, brightly lighted corridor with green walls and a gleaming tile floor. "What do you mean, save my life? You seem to delight in just the opposite in this place, from what I hear."

The doctor made an impatient noise. "Listen to any story you want; *I* don't care. If you want to believe all the scare stories and smears about our work, that's your privilege. But realize that even at best, they're only half-true, and most of them are pure fabrication. This business of bloodthirstiness, for instance. It's just plain not true. Sometimes I wish it were. My biggest headache around here is trying to arrange optimum conditions for the success of any experiment we do. By 'optimum' I mean the best of all possible conditions from several standpoints. From the standpoint of what we're trying to learn, of course, the experiment itself, that is. Also from the standpoint of the researcher. But above all, and even overriding all these other considerations, we want optimum conditions for recovery of the experimental animals—you, in this case."

"But we're still just experimental animals," Jeff said bitterly, "as far as you're concerned."

"Not *just* experimental animals," the doctor said. "You're *the* experimental animals. Working with human beings isn't the same as working with cats and dogs and monkeys—far from it. Cats and dogs are far stronger and tougher, far more durable than humans. There isn't a more resilient animal alive than a well-seasoned, beaten-up old alley tomcat, which is why cats are so useful for so much of our preliminary work. But much as we may dislike it, they're basically expendable. If something goes wrong, that's too bad, but we've learned something. If we have to sacrifice a dog or a cat to learn what we need to know, we can do it without too many tears. But we don't feel quite the same way about human beings."

"I'm relieved to hear that," said Jeff sourly. "That makes me feel a whole lot better."

"Well, I'm not trying to be facetious," Schiml retorted. "I mean it. We're not butchers. We're responsible for a certain number of human casualties in the work we're doing, yes. But that doesn't mean we have any less regard for human life than anyone else. More, if anything. When you're responsible for the care of something irreplaceable and precious, you do everything humanly possible to safeguard and protect it." He paused to look at Jeff. "Why do you think this great heap of buildings was built in the first place? Just to keep the construction crews in business? If we didn't think human life was worth fighting for there wouldn't be any Hoffman Medical Research Center. Nor any Mercy Men, either."

Jeff scratched his head, confused. He hadn't thought of it quite that way before, and Dr. Schiml certainly sounded convicing. "Well, that seems to make sense," he said, "but what does it really mean as far as the Mercy Men are concerned? What do you actually *do* to protect them?"

"A lot more than meets the eye," Schiml retorted. "For one thing, we study every human being we use for any kind of experimental work. We try to dig out his strengths and his weaknesses, both physical and mental, before we let him commit himself. We want to know how he reacts to what; how fast he recuperates; how much physical punishment his body is actually equipped to take; how far his mental resilience extends. When we know these things about a given man, we can try to fit him into the particular research program that will give him the best possible chance of coming out in one piece, and at the same time will fulfill a research need important enough to justify the risk in the first place. A lot of volunteers don't fill the bill, one way or the other: either they haven't got the stamina to have a plausible chance in the spot where we need them, or else they have the stamina but don't happen to lend themselves well to one of our programs. In either case, they are gently but firmly escorted to the door, or, if possible, rehabilitated and retested. And considering the human wreckage we have coming in here as applicants, even that is a postive benefit. We probably don't use one out of twenty who apply by the time we're through." The doctor shook his head. "Believe me, nobody around here finds any delight in jeopardizing human life or safety. We keep it to the barest possible minimum."

They turned down a side corridor and entered a small office. Schiml motioned Jeff to a chair, then sat down himself behind a desk and began sorting through several stacks of data cards. Jeff waited in silence. Finally the doctor picked up the telephone and punched a call code. "Gabe?" he said when the answer light blinked. "I've got him here. Better come on down." Closing out the call, he leaned back and with a sigh loosened the surgical gown around his neck.

Jeff watched him, still puzzling over what he had just said. Schiml had seemed so matter-of-fact and forthright it didn't seem possible he could be lying. But something was still wrong with the picture. "This sounds like a great setup for you doctors and researchers," he said finally. "But what's it leading to? What good is it doing? Oh, I know, it increases knowledge of men's minds and all that, but how does it help the man in the street right now? How does it help anyone, in the long run? It must take a fantastic budget to do what you say. How do you ever get government backing, with the money mess they're facing in Washington?"

Schiml smiled. "You've got the cart before the horse, I'm afraid, just like most people. Financial support? Listen, my friend: the government is running itself bankrupt just to keep our research going. Literally bankrupt. And why do you suppose all that money is being appropriated? Because the government knows that if our work doesn't pay off very, very soon, there isn't going to be any government left, that's why."

Jeff stared at him. "Are you serious?"

"Very serious."

"But why? What's happening?"

The doctor sighed. "I wish I could tell you, for sure. We don't really know. All we know is that for a century or more something bad has been going on—not just in this country but all over the world. Something—some creeping sickness, some fundamental decay—has been gnawing away at the very roots of our civilization. We don't know what it is, exactly, but it involves human minds and human bodies on a massive scale. It involves mental illness. The index figures we report publicly don't begin to reflect the real increase that we know of. If we told the true story it would cause world-wide panic."

He looked up at Jeff who was staring at him with his jaw sagging. "The government knows how grave the situation is," Schiml went on. "They've known for a long time. They've watched it grow. There's a sort of hideous fascination to it. Like watching a snake swallow a rabbit: you can't believe what you're seeing, but you can't take your eyes off it, either. Well, we had to prove to the government that it was happening at all, show them time and again until at last somebody listened to us, or else they just couldn't ignore it any longer, but finally they saw it. They've seen other aspects of it: the business instability, the bank runs and stock market dives, the drifters crowding the streets, the noise riots breaking out without warning in places you'd least expect them, people going into mass panic from the sheer pressure and noise in the big cities. The government saw it, all right, but it took statistics to prove to them that there was a pattern and to show where the pattern was leading. After that, there wasn't any question about financial support. What's happening has to be identified and stopped."

Schiml stood up, stretched, and poured coffee from a vendor in the wall. "We don't know for sure what we're fighting, but we're certain the answer lies in human behavior. We're working against a creeping disease affecting men's minds, and that means we have to use men—human minds—to help us fight it. So we have the Mercy Men, men and women with no more capacity for mercy than cornered rats, people with no interest nor concern with *what* they are doing or what it may be accomplishing. People interested in one thing only:

how much they'll get paid for having their brains jogged loose."

Schiml let this sink in and continued angrily. "Well, we don't care whom we have, as long as the volunteers fill the bill. We'll take addicts, condemned murderers, drifters, trash from the skid row gutters—anybody who'll come. They're here for big money, but they're here on errands of mercy just the same, maybe even in spite of themselves. And we take them because they're the ones who can be bought, and then we guard them for all we're worth so that somehow we can win this fight. And anybody can qualify for testing." He took a deep breath. "Even you."

Jeff's hands shook as he sipped his coffee. The office door opened and a small man came in. He had dark hair and thick glasses, and wore a doctor's whites. Jeff rubbed his chest, feeling the stiff file card still concealed inside his shirt. "All right," he said hoarsely. "So you're talking about me. When do we get started?"

## V

THE DRESSING room was cramped, and reeked of anesthetic. Jeff walked in, followed by Dr. Schiml and the other doctor, and started to remove his shoes. "This is Gabriel," Schiml said, indicating his myopic colleague. "He'll start you off with a complete physical examination, including a neurological. Come on into the examining room here as soon as you're undressed." And with that the two doctors disappeared through swinging doors into an inner room.

Jeff removed his shirt and trousers swiftly. He carefully folded the file card and stuffed it under the inner sole of his right shoe. It was not exactly the place he would have chosen to hide it, given a choice, but it would have to do. Anyway, Schiml must not have seen him take it; not once during their conversation had the doctor even glanced at his shirt front. If he *had* seen him stick it in there, his self-control was super-human. Nor, for that matter, had Schiml made any mention of the dice. Jeff paused at the thought. Odd thing, those dice. Coincidence? Impossible. Jeff shrugged, gave his shoes a final pat, tossed his clothing in a pile on top of them, and pushed through the door into the next room.

It was a huge room with a dome in the ceiling. A dozen partitions separated one section from another. One end looked like a classroom—blackboards occupied a whole wall. Another section was filled with gymnasium equipment—parallel bars, rings, a trapeze, a trampoline. The doctors were waiting in a corner that was obviously outfitted as a medical examining room; the tables were covered with a crisp green sheeting, and the walls held glass cabinets full of green-wrapped bundles and instruments. Schiml sat on the edge of a desk, watching Jeff closely as he lit his pipe. Dr. Gabriel motioned Jeff to the examining table.

It was the most rigorous, painstaking physical examination Jeff had ever had. The doctor poked and probed him from head to toe, listening, prodding, thumping, auscultating, snapping retinal photos, recording pore patterns. After half an hour he motioned Jeff onto another table and started going over him with a rubber hammer, tapping him sharply in dozens of areas, eliciting a most disconcerting variety of muscular jerks and twitches. Presently the hammer was replaced by a small electrode with which the doctor probed and tested, causing involuntary spasms of muscle groups in Jeff's back and arms and thighs. Finally Dr. Gabriel relaxed, sat Jeff down in a soft chair, and retired to a small portable instrument cabinet nearby.

"Is that all?" Jeff asked.

Dr. Schiml laughed. "That was just to establish crude base lines," he said. "We haven't even started the real testing yet." He paused and set down his pipe. "Any questions before we begin?"

Jeff just sat there, feeling foolish. Any questions? He almost laughed aloud. He was so tense he could barely hold still; his mind was full of conjecture, wild ridiculous guesses of what they would discover in the testing, of what the results might be. Suppose they learned about the dice? Suppose they found out that he was a fraud, here on a private mission all his own, with no interest whatever in anything *they* might be planning? If he kept his wits about him, maybe he could continue to fool them, but what if they rendered him unconscious, knocked him out, used drugs? He groped for some way of stalling things, slowing down the procedure of testing and assignment so he could have more time to complete his own mission before the chips were down. But he knew already he must have aroused suspicions. Schiml was nobody's fool; certainly he, at least, must have suspected that all the cards were not on the table. Yet Schiml seemed deliberately determined to overlook Jeff's blunders, and now the wheels were moving him more and more swiftly to the critical moment when he would have to sign a release and accept an assignment, or else reveal his real purpose for being here. If he were to find Conroe at all, he would have to find him before that moment came. He stared at Schiml, and shook his head. "No. No questions, I guess."

The doctor shrugged. "All right," he said, tiredly. "You'll have a whole series of tests of all kinds now: physical stamina, mental alertness, reaction time, intelligence, sanity—everything we might ever need to know. You can cooperate or you can fight—it's up to you. But understand one thing. All of these tests are subjective; they depend on responses you report or demonstrate. All of them will tell us about you as a person—how you think, how you react, how you handle trouble. Its des-

peratelv essential stuff, if you want to survive the sort
of work we do." He paused for a long moment. "So
you'd be smart to stick to the truth. No embellishments,
no fancy stuff. We can't keep you from falsifying and
faking if you insist, but you're cutting your own throat
if you do. That's all."

Jeff blinked, shifting in his seat uneasily. *Don't worry
about that,* he thought. *I won't be around long enough
for it to matter.* But all the same, the sober words were
far from comforting. If only he could maintain the fraud
throughout the testing, keep his wits about him as the
tests progressed, he could get back to his search while
they were busy evaluating results. But if they moved
fast, he would *really* be in trouble. He watched Dr.
Schiml take out a pile of papers from the desk. Then
came a rapid-fire barrage of questions: family history,
personal history, history of family disease and personal
illness. The questions were swift and businesslike, and
Jeff felt his muscles relaxing as he sat back, answering
almost automatically. Then: "Ever been hypnotized?"

Something in Jeff's mind froze. "No," he snapped.

Schiml's eyes widened. "That's too bad. Part of the
testing ought to be done under hypnosis, for your sake,
and for the sake of speed. Unless you have some particular objection."

"It won't work," Jeff lied swiftly, searching for ex-
cuses. "It's been tried. Some kind of block against it,
I guess. My father had a block against it too."

Schiml shrugged. "Usually those blocks are easy to
get around. A little drug-induced sleep, and—"

"No." Jeff said. "Lets forget the hypnosis."

"It'll make the tests a hundred per cent easier on you,"
Schiml persisted. "Some of them are pretty exhausting,
and some take an awfully long time without hypnotic
recovery aid. Naturally, we keep all information strictly
confidential."

"No dice," Jeff said, suddenly and irrationally tense.
"No hypnosis."

Schiml shrugged and glanced over at Dr. Gabriel. "Okay, Gabe. You heard the man."

The doctor nodded. "It's his funeral." He rolled a small, shiny paneled instrument over to Jeff's side, unhooked a pair of earphones. "Maybe you'll change your mind. Meanwhile, we'll start on a few less strenuous things. This is a hearing test. Very simple; you just listen, mark down the signals you hear. Keep your eye on the eye-piece; it records visio-audio correlation times, tells us how soon after you hear a word the visual image forms in your mind." He snapped the earphones over Jeff's head, and moved a printed answer sheet in front of him on the desk. And then the earphones started talking.

There was a long series of words, gradually becoming softer and softer. Jeff marked the sheet swiftly, gradually forgetting his surroundings, turning his full attention to the test. The doctors retired to the other side of the room, talking to each other in low whispers, until he could no longer hear them; he could hear only the low, insistent whispering in the earphones.

Presently, imperceptibly, the words seemed to grow louder again, but he was only vaguely aware of that. He seemed to have lost track of what they were saying, somehow. For a moment he thought his attention had strayed, and he listened intently to pick up the thread, his eyes fixed on the cool pearl-gray screen of the vision screen, his fingers poised to mark down the words. But listen as he would, he couldn't quite make out the syllables.

Because they were nonsense syllables, syllables with no meaning. His eyes opened wide, a bolt of suspicion shooting through him, and his hands gripped the arms of the chair as he began to rise.

The light exploded in his eyes, blue-white agonizing in its brilliance. He let out a stifled cry. Struggling, he tried to rise from the chair, but he was blinded by the piercing beam and something was holding his arms and legs. And then he felt the needle bite his arm, and the nonsense words in his ears straightened out into meaningful phrases, and a soft, soothing voice was saying, "Relax . . . relax . . . sit back and relax . . . relax and rest . . ."

Slowly, a sense of warmth crept through his body, and he felt his muscles relax, just as the voice instructed, easing him gently back into the chair, and soon his mind was free of fear, and worry, and suspicion, and he was breathing gently, and then sleeping with the peaceful ease of a newborn child.

## VI

HE KNEW, later, that it could never have been done without hypnosis. Schiml had lied, at least as far as that was concerned. Within broad limits, he knew, the human body was capable of doing whatever it thought it could. But the human body could hardly be blamed if convention had long since decided that exertion was bad, that straining to the limit of endurance was unhealthy, that approaching, even obliquely, the safe limits of human resiliency was equivalent to approaching death with arms extended. That convention had so declared was well known to the researchers at the Hoffman Center.

But it was also known that the human body, under the soothing suggestion of hypnosis, could be carried up to the normal margin of safety, and beyond. If necessary, it could be carried almost to the actual physical breaking point without stir, without a flicker of protest, without a sign of fear. These were the conditions that were critically needed in testing the Mercy Men. Yet, though hypnosis was necessary, the volunteers who came to the Mercy Men invariably rejected hypnosis, whether through fear of divulging some secret of their past, through distrust of the doctors and the testing in the center, or through plain, ordinary orneriness. No one knew their motives, or even cared; but later, when he knew what had happened, Jeff suspected those who needed hypnosis the most for testing rejected it the most vehemently.

Not that it mattered. The Hoffman Center had not been around all this time without learning a few fundamentals—such as how to hypnotize a man against his will.

Jeff Meyer would have been angry if he had known. He might well have been furious, because Jeff, among other things, was afraid. As it was, it made very little difference *how* he felt, because the quiet voice in his ear told him not to be afraid, and so he was not afraid. His mind was in a relaxed, happy haze, and he felt his body half lifted, half led across the room to the first section of the testing room. Even now there was a tiny, sharp-voiced sentinel tucked away in a corner of his mind, shouting out a message of alertness and fear to Jeff, but he laughed, sinking deeper into the peacefulness of his walking slumber. Dr. Gabriel was talking to him, quietly and smoothly, giving simple instructions, taking him in a few hours through the paces of a testing series that would otherwise have taken long, hard days to complete, and very possibly left him mentally crippled at the end without the recuperative buffer of hypnosis to help him.

First he was dressed in soft flannel clothing and moved into the gymnasium. Recorders were attached to his legs, arms and throat; then he was formally introduced to the treadmill, and asked to run on it until he collapsed. He smiled, and obliged, running as though the furies were nipping at his heels until his face went purple and his muscles knotted. At last he fell down, unable to continue.

This happened after fifteen minutes of top-limit running. Then came five minutes of recuperation under suggestion: *Your heart is beating slower, you're breathing softly and deeply . . . relaxing . . . relaxing . . . relaxing.* Someone took his arm, then, and he was off again, this time on the old, reliable Harvard step-test, jumping up on the chair, and back down, repeatedly. He did this until once again he lay panting on the floor, hardly able to move as his pulse and respiration changes were carefully and tenderly recorded.

Next in line came a lively handball game; he was given a small, hard-rubber ball, and asked to engage in a game of catch with a machine stationed in a corner of the room. The machine played hard. It also played dirty, spinning the ball around and hurling it at Jeff with such incredible rapidity that he was forced to abandon all thinking. When he reached out for it, instinctively, the ball burned his fingers; he hurled it away, only to have it hurled back again twice as fast. Soon he moved as automatically as a machine, catching, hurling, his mind ignoring the aching and swelling in his fingers as the ball struck and struck and struck—

On to the trampoline then, like any trampoline, except that this one . . . *whoing!* . . . seemed to have an energy of its own . . . *whoing!* . . . throwing him higher and harder each time . . . *whoing!* . . . no time to think or look . . . *whoing!* . . . guard your neck, Jeff . . . *whoing!* . . . you'll snap it next time . . . *whoing!* . . . get control . . . *whoing!* . . . control . . . *whoing!* . . . *control.* . . .

Later, as he lay bruised and inert, the soft voice whispered. A small ladder was rolled in. He listened carefully to instructions, and then ran up and down the ladder until he fell fainting from the top. He rested gently on the floor while blood samples were taken from his arm. Now he sat, staring dully at the floor (*relax, Jeff . . . take a rest . . . sleep quietly, Jeff . . . you'll be ready to dig in and fight in a minute . . . just relax . . .*). Several people were about; one brought him a heavy, sugary drink, lukewarm and revolting. He drank it down, slopping it on his shirt front. Then he sat benignly while further blood samples were drawn. Finally he was allowed to take a drink of cool water, and to sit staring at his feet, uninterrupted, for five whole minutes for recuperation before the next stage of the testing commenced.

This time there were lights in three long columns, extending as far as he could see. Some were blinking, some shone with steady intensity, while others were dark. "Call the columns one, two and three," said Dr. Gabriel, close by, his voice soft with patience. "Record the position of the lights as you see them now. Then when the signal sounds, start recording every light change you see in all three columns. *Fast*, Jeff, as fast as you can!"

The eye is a wonderful instrument of precision, capable of detecting an incredible variety of movements and changes simultaneously, delicate enough to distinguish, if necessary, each and every individual frame of a motion picture film that flickers so swiftly before it on the screen. Jeff's fingers moved, his pencil recorded, swiftly going from column one to column two, and on to column three, back and forth, faster and faster until the test was over.

Then on to the next test.

Surface electrodes were attached to each of his ten toes and ten fingers, with each electrode corresponding to a pushbutton on the panel before him. "Listen closely, Jeff. I'll tell you just once: your right first toe corresponds to left thumb, right second toe to right index finger. (Wonderful stuff, hypno-palamine, only one repetition to learn!) When you feel a shock in a toe, press the button for the corresponding finger. Ready, now, Jeff, as fast as you can."

Shock, press, shock, press—Jeff's mind was still, silent, a blank, an open circuit carrying reaction signals through without hindrance, without modulation, at incredible speed. Another round done, and on to the next.

Doctor Schiml's pale face loomed up from some distant place. "Everything all right, Gabe?"

"Going fine, fine. Smooth as can be."

"No snags anywhere?"·

"No, no snags. None that I can see—yet."

# VII

"I NEED SOME coffee," Jeff said. "I've about had it."

Dr. Gabriel relaxed, carried a cup of black coffee over to Jeff and smiled. Jeff noticed that his eyes failed to focus and he overshot the cup reaching for it.

"How do you feel, Jeff?"

"Fine, fine."

"Still got a lot to do."

A flicker of fear in Jeff's mind. "Fine. Only I hope—"

"Yes?"

"—hope we finish pretty soon. I can't keep it up much longer."

"Sleepy?"

"Yeah, sleepy."

"Well, we'll have everything on punched cards for Tilly in a couple more hours. All the factors about you that this testing will unearth would take a research staff five hundred years to integrate down to the point where it would mean anything. With Tilly it takes five minutes. She doesn't make mistakes, either."

"Nice Tilly."

"And then when the results come through, and you're assigned and sign your release, you'll be on your way to the big money."

Again the flicker of fear, deeper this time. His head seemed full of cotton wool, he couldn't seem to think clearly. "Money," he repeated, vaguely puzzled. "Oh, yes."

After five minutes' rest there were more tests, then still more. Hear a sound, punch a button. See a picture, record it. Test after endless test, dozens of records, as he grew tired, tired. Body-tired, mind-tired. Then into the bright, gleaming room, up onto the green-draped table. "No pain, Jeff, nothing to worry about. Be over in just a minute—"

His eyes caught the slender wicked-looking trefine, like a dentist's drill, heard the buzz of the motor, felt the vibration above his forehead and at his temples, but there was no reaction, no pain. Then he felt the odd tingling in his arms and legs as the small electro-encephalograph leads entered his skull through the tiny drilled holes. He watched with dull eyes as the little lights on the control board nearby began blinking on and off, on and off, in a hectic, nervous pattern, registering individual brain cell activity onto super-sensitive stroboscopic film which fed down to Tilly automatically, for analysis. The trefine holes were plugged up again, and his head was tightly taped, and he was moved back into another room for another five minutes' recovery.

Schiml was there. "Have you hit the ink blots yet?" he asked impatiently.

"Not yet, Rog. Take it easy, we're coming along. Ink blots and intelligence runs next, and so on."

"Sorry. Don't let me rush you. But that's where we'll hit pay dirt, you know."

Something stirred deep in Jeff's mind, even through the soothing delusions of hypnosis. Something in his mind drew back at the first sign of the strange, colored forms on the cards. He felt himself cringing as though some malignant force was closing in and there was no place to hide.

"Just look at them, Jeff," Dr. Gabriel said softly. "Tell me what you see."

"No! Take them away."

"What's that? Easy, Jeff, they're just ink blots. Relax and take a look."

Jeff was on his feet, backing away from the desk. "Take them away. Get me out of here. Go away—"

"Jeff!" The voice was sharp, commanding. "Sit down, Jeff."

Jeff sank back down in the seat, gingerly, his eyes wary. The doctor moved his hand and Jeff jerked away, his teeth chattering.

"What's the trouble, Jeff?"

"I—I don't like—those—cards—"

"But why not? They're just pieces of cardboard."

Jeff frowned and squinted at the cards. He scratched his head in perplexity. Slowly he relaxed in the chair. He didn't even notice as the web-belt restrainers eased up to close over his arms and legs, tightened down. "Now look at the pictures, Jeff. Tell me what you see."

His perplexity grew, but he looked, and talked, slowly, hoarsely. A dog's head, a little gnome, a big red bat.

"Gently, Jeff. Nothing to be afraid of. Relax, man, relax. . . ."

The word-association tests came now, half an hour of words and answers, while the sense of helpless panic grew in Jeff's mind, gathering steadily. There was a feeling of horrible anticipation; he knew something dreadful was coming as sure as hour followed hour. Suddenly he was aware of the web restrainers pressing his wrists as the doctor shot words at him for association response, and he began trembling.

Dr. Schiml was back again, still concerned, his eyes bright. "Going all right, Gabe?"

"Dunno, Rog. Something funny with the ink blots. Take a look there. Word association is all screwed up too. Can't spot what it is, but there's something funny—"

"Rest him a minute and reinforce the 'palamine. Probably got a powerful vitality opposing it."

Dr. Gabriel nodded, and another needle nibbled Jeff's

arm briefly. The doctor walked to the desk, took out a little square plastic box. He dropped the cards out into his hand. They were the cards Dr. Schiml had had on his desk at the first interview, plain-backed cards with bright red symbols on their faces.

Dr. Gabriel held them out for Jeff to see. "Modified Rhine cards," he said softly. "Four different symbols, Jeff. Look closely. There's a square, a circle—"

*It was like a jolting electric current, ripping through Jeff's mind without mercy, like a red-hot spike driving through his head. He saw those cards and something exploded like napalm in his brain.*

"My God, *hold him!*"

Jeff screamed, wide awake, his eyes bulging in terror. With an animal roar he wrenched at his restrainers, ripped them out of the raw wood, and plunged across the room in blind, terrified flight and struck the solid brick wall full face. He hit with a sickening thud, pounded at the wall with his fists, screaming again and again. And then he collapsed, his nose bleeding, his face scraped, his fingers raw with the nails broken.

As he slid into merciful unconsciousness he heard himself blubbering, "He killed my father . . . killed him . . . killed him . . . killed him . . . killed him. . . ."

## Part Three

## THE TRAP

## I

HOURS LATER Jeff Meyer stirred. He tried to move his arm and almost cried out in pain. His chest seemed to burn as he breathed. When he opened his eyes, a violent headache began pounding. Even so, he moved, trying to orient himself. He was back in his room. He recognized the furnishings, saw the empty bed across from him. He reached up to feel the bandages on his head and face.

He listened. At first there was only silence. Then he heard the harsh, gurgling breathing of the man in the next room, the man called Tinker, whose fate as a Mercy Man had not yet quite been sealed and who breathed on, shallowly, breaking the deadly stillness.

*What had happened?*

Jeff sat bolt upright in the dim light, ignoring the pain in his chest and neck. His face felt as if someone had pounded it with a hammer. What had happened? Why was he bandaged? What had happened that had left him, even now, virtually paralyzed with fear?

He stared across at the opposite bed. Of course. He had been in the file room, and Schiml had caught him there and taken him down for testing. Simple at first, memory clear, and then without warning a blazing bright light, nonsense words whispered in his ear, a needle . . . and then *nothing*.

But what about the card he had stolen . . . the data

card on Conroe? Jeff rolled out of bed, groped frantically for his shoes. He tore the inner sole out, and found the crumpled card. He sighed in relief. Whatever had happened, they hadn't found that. They didn't know he had it. But what *had* happened? Slowly, other things began coming back. Vague, fuzzy memories of endless, grueling tests. Dr. Gabriel peering at him through thick glasses, handing him a cup of coffee when he begged for a rest. Something about ink blots, and . . . something else. And then the sound of himself screaming as he had broken free of the restraints and struck the wall like a ten-ton truck.

*When?* How long ago? He stared at his watch, hardly believing his eyes. It said 7:00 A.M. It had been almost 1:00 A.M. when they had first taken him down to Dr. Gabriel. It *couldn't* be seven in the morning again, unless he had slept almost around the clock. He shook the watch suspiciously, but it was still running. Whatever had happened with Dr. Gabriel had thrown him so hard that he had slept for at least twenty-two hours, maybe more. And in the course of that time. . . .

The horrible loss struck him suddenly. More than forty-eight hours gone since he had seen Conroe on the stairs. All that time for Conroe to conceal himself better! Jeff sank back on the bed, groaning. Previous time lost, too muih time. The man was here, somewhere, among the Mercy Men, but to find him now, after so much time . . . how? And on top of that, his *own* lost time, too much time. The man was here, some- testing, the computer called Tilly would process the data without waste of time, and the next step would be assignment, and a release to sign, the point of no return.

Behind everything else, buried deep in his mind, was a phantom he couldn't pin down. What, really, was going on in his mind that he couldn't control? Why the jolting shock, during the testing? Why had he torn loose and driven himself blindly into a solid wall at the sight of a few pasteboard cards? Why that uncontrollable wave of blind, unreasoning fear? *And why was that same fear invariably associated with Paul Conroe?*

Because it was. Always. He hadn't realized it before, but now there was no question. His nightmares, his obsessive search for Conroe after their confrontation on the library steps, his single-minded determination to confront that man again no matter what it cost . . . all were bound up with some terrible, nameless fear he couldn't even comprehend.

He sighed. He need help, and he knew it. He needed it badly. He thought longingly of Barney. If only *he* were here. He and Em had helped, once before, when he was ready to leave the hospital and needed help. They had come forward and said, "We'll take this boy, he's an orphan, he needs care." With them he had grown up; Em so gentle, and Barney always rock solid. Em had died from that virus, just when he had left school to hunt down Conroe, and then there had been the long night when he tried to explain to Barney what had happened, why he had to hunt down a man he didn't even know. Barney never understood, but Barney had joined him, nevertheless, until Conroe had slipped away to this place.

But Barney wasn't here now; there was no Barney to rely on. Here, in this cesspool of hatred and selfishness, he needed help more than he had ever needed it before in his life: help to track down this phantom fear, help to corner it, to find out what it meant. But the only ones he could ask for help now were those around him, the Mercy Men themselves. And he needed their help, if only to escape becoming one of them.

## II

JEFF DOZED, unable to fight down his dreadful lethargy. Hours later he woke, listening. Something had changed. He felt an aura of tension in the room, a subtle suggestion of something gone terribly wrong. Slowly he forced himself up on his elbow, peering about the room. Something had happened, just before he woke. He listened, intently, to the deathly stillness.

Then he knew what it was. The breathing in the next room had stopped.

He lay back, his heart pounding. Death had come, then. Waiting in the wings, Death had heard his cue, and moved on-stage to claim one man who would never see the big money he had been promised. Jeff didn't know how or why, but he had felt Death pass close by, and he knew, instinctively, that the whole unit would know it, very soon, without a single word being said. Jeff hadn't prayed very often, these past three years, but he prayed now, an old prayer. *For the souls of the faithful, departed.* And for the first time he felt a sudden kinship with the Mercy Men, a depth of understanding he shared with them. And deep down, a depth of fear he knew that he must share with them also.

He rolled onto his side, painfully, and stared into the darkness for long minutes before he fell again into a fitful sleep.

## III

SOMEWHERE across the room someone was talking, a muffled up-and-down rumble of sound. Slowly Jeff struggled up out of his recurring nightmare, back to the stuffy, dimly lit room. The voices (there were more than one) had been going on for some time, he was certain of that. How long had he slept? How much more time had he lost?

The voices gave no clue. Oddly, he felt certain they would stop if he appeared to be awake, so he lay very still, keeping his breathing slow and steady, half listening. It was hard to pay attention, though; every muscle ached and his mind was still fresh with the nightmare.

It had been very sharp this time, clear, stark images, as if spotlighted on a stage. The same dream, of course, the same face, the same dreadful, mindless fear. But this time the dream had taken more coherent shape, its form far clearer and more unmistakable than before.

This time, he had dreamed about his first real encounter with Conroe, on the library steps. He had gone through it all, second for second, just as it had happened. And when he had actually seen Conroe's face time seemed to have frozen and he had felt again the violent shock multiplied a thousand times.

*Like the shock and panic he had felt in the testing room!* No, more than just *like* it: the *same, identical* panic. . . .

The voices across the room were louder. Gradually snatches and phrases came clear as he lay there motionless, his eyes still closed. One voice was a woman's. Blackie, arguing violently. And there was no mistaking the Nasty Frenchman's nasal twang. The third voice was familiar, a gruff rumble, but he couldn't place it. Jeff opened his eyes a crack, moved his head slightly in order to see the people huddled at the table across the room.

The third one was Harpo, the huge bald-headed giant from the game room. Blackie's voice was sharp and pleading, echoing the Nasty Frenchman's angry protest. Harpo's heavy bass rumbled an adamant undertone in half-whispered discussion. Suddenly Jeff caught a phrase or two, and stiffened, wide awake.

"I say find out who it is and do something about it," the Nasty Frenchman was insisting angrily. "Accidents happen, and a corpse can't snatch a job away from us. Sit around a while longer and it'll be too late." His face was flushed as he glared at Harpo. "Look, you stupid ox, we're going to be out of it completely if we don't move! Can't you see that? If they make this switch we'll be off the payroll! Just ditched to sit around hopefully waiting. And if its *really* hot we could wait ten years. Well, I don't want to wait. The job Schiml promised me would pay two hundred grand with practically no risk. I'm not going to let some greenhorn walk in and cut me out of it, just because he's got Schiml stirred up."

Harpo's voice was placating. "Maybe you're daydreaming, Jacques. Maybe they won't switch any jobs at all. You've got nothing but rumors to go on."

"I saw the report, I tell you! It was signed by Schiml himself."

Harpo looked up at him. "You mean you actually saw Schiml's signature on it?"

"That's what I'm trying to get through that thick skull of yours," the Frenchman said, exasperated. "I *saw* the signature, I read the report. I'm to be taken off assignment and so are you. We're just being by-passed, all of a sudden, because somebody has walked in here off the street and gotten them all excited."

Harpo grunted. "ESP again, I suppose."

"Of course. What else would get Schiml excited?"

"Well . . . so why worry? He'll kick it soon enough. He always does. Look, Jacques, about once every two years Schiml goes off on one of these spook hunts, and nothing ever develops, and pretty soon things are back to the routine again. Extrasensory perception." The big man snorted. "Have *you* ever seen anybody with extrasensory powers? Well, neither have I. Look, let's face it, Schiml runs things here, and ESP is his pet baby. He'd give his left arm at the shoulder to find *proof* that ESP even exists in any form. He believes in it, he *wants* to prove it. And every now and then he's going to have a try at it. It's one of the facts of life around this place. So why get excited?"

"Because this time he may have the genuine article," Blackie said gloomily. "He's actually got a solid lead. From what I hear, this new guy is a phenomenon, whoever he is. Hit top scores on the cards, the highest they've ever recorded. And he can do things, too, like making the paper peel off the walls just by looking at them, or setting fires without any matches, or closing up open wounds in ten minutes."

"So you hear stories! Well, who can believe what you hear around here?" Harpo was scornful, but he sounded uneasy. "If there was anything really solid, anything we could put our fingers on, I'd listen, believe me. I don't want to get scratched from a job any more than you do. But you've got no proof, nothing but a lot of wild stories. Well, you can't go around fighting stories."

Slowly Jeff sat up on the edge of the bed. "What kind of proof are you looking for?" he asked.

Harpo stared at him, as though seeing a ghost. Blackie started violently. Then, after a glance at the others, Harpo said, "Any kind of proof."

"Then take a look at this," Jeff said. He reached down for his shoes, pulled the file card on Conroe out of its hiding place and tossed it on the table. "Look, but don't touch," he said. "I'd hate to lose that."

## IV

BLACKIE WAS on her feet, startled and nervous. "We didn't know you were awake," she said. "You look like they really gave you the works."

"That's . . . one way to put it."

Blackie nodded. "Testing is always rough. I'd hoped maybe they'd missed you after they came looking for you. I tried to steer them away, but then when you didn't come back I figured they'd caught up." She handed Jeff a cup of coffee and pointed to the file card. "You actually got that out of the file without being spotted?"

"That's right. Hid it in my shoe." Their eyes met for a moment, and he caught a look of warning, a silent helpless appeal. He nodded briefly. She hadn't told the others about their battle over the dice. "I think that card answers a lot of questions," he said.

Harpo's eyes were suspicious. "How do you know this is the man?"

"Because I chased him in here, that's why." Jeff's voice was angry. "I didn't know he'd been here before, and I sure didn't know there was any connection with ESP, but I know the man. He came in here the day I did, trying to get away from me." He paused. "I think he thought I might kill him if I caught him."

Harpo stared at the card, then at Jeff. "You mean you've got a private beef with this man?"

"That's right," Jeff said. "Tell them, Blackie. Tell them why I'm here."

Blackie told them. They listened with widening eyes, and the room was silent as a tomb. Then Harpo gave a long, low whistle. "And I thought I'd heard everything! You're spooky, man. You're just plain unhinged if you come walking into this place merely to *talk* to a man."

"That's my business," Jeff said.

"But you're on thin ice. *Very* thin ice. If they tested you last night, they could be assigning you any time, handing you a release to sign. And once a release is signed, my friend, you don't leave."

"I know all that," Jeff snapped. "Can't you see there's no time for bickering now? This is the man I'm looking for. He's also the one *you're* looking for, the one with ESP who has Schiml and his boys so excited! It's all right here on the card!"

Harpo's eyes were narrow. "Any proof besides this card that this Conroe is really the man we want?"

Jeff considered for a minute. "Not proof, exactly, but some suggestive evidence, at least. I've been trying to catch up with this man for three years. I've had plenty of good help and I've spent plenty of money . . . my father left a small fortune when he died. I've had some of the best private skip-tracers in North America working with me for weeks and months on end, and we've never pinned this guy down. Not once. We've almost caught him a dozen times. We've been right on his heels until he's been run ragged, but we've never actually been able to set up a trap that held, when the chips were down."

Harpo blinked. "So? I don't follow you."

"Well, doesn't that seem a little odd? We've come so close we couldn't miss, time and again, but then we've missed after all. Too many times for coincidence. More like a pattern—some factor that has been giving Conroe advance warning, time after time, so he's been able to slip out of our traps. Some factor like precognition, for instance."

There was a long silence. Then the Nasty Frenchman was on his feet, overflowing with excitement. "He's right, it *does* add up!" he said. "And this would be one

Schiml would give anything to work with. He'd scratch a dozen other programs for the chance. Well, if we move fast enough, we can see to it he doesn't have this wonder boy to work with. We're off the payroll, as it stands. But we can get back on in a hurry if his wonder boy turns up dead or something."

"Not dead!" Jeff said sharply. "I want time with that man."

"Oh, sure," the Nasty Frenchman grinned. "We understand that. You want him first so he can talk, and that's okay. We can even help encourage him to talk, if he's a little bit reluctant." He gave a malicious laugh. "You can count on us, boy, but when you're through with him he's ours."

"Just how do you plan to bring this off?" Harpo broke in.

"Nothing simpler," the Nasty Frenchman said. "Our friend here wants him first, he knows him best. We'll let him find him. We'll help, we'll cover, help keep him pinned once he's found. Right, Jeff?"

"Right," Jeff said, suddenly fiercely eager. "You help me find him, he's yours when I get through."

Harpo considered for a long moment. Then he nodded and poured more coffee. "Okay," he said softly. "You've got a deal. Let's talk plans."

V

It went very smoothly, then. Jeff sat forward listening more than he talked, as the hopelessness and despair of an hour before seemed to vanish. Here was an incredible break; these people knew the layout of the place, they knew where and how to hunt. This was the help he needed so desperately to find Conroe, to pin him down at last. As they talked he heard a corner of his mind telling him that he was a fool, that the Nasty Frenchman couldn't be trusted to give him five minutes' time with the man once he was caught, that even at best he was signing Conroe's death warrant by throwing in with this team. But he closed his mind to the thought, refused to let it dampen his elation. *That was Conroe's headache, wasn't it? He'd had plenty of chances to come forward before without facing any threat. Now let him do his own worrying.* For a moment Jeff was jolted by his own cold-bloodedness . . . *this isn't right, Jeff, this isn't you* . . . but he thrust that aside too.

Harpo was fingering the file card thoughtfully. "These dates must have some meaning. If you were hunting him, didn't you know he was here at these times?"

Jeff shook his head. "No. Oh, there were times when we lost him for days, even weeks. But we had no hint he'd ever come *here.*"

"Strange." Harpo looked at him. "Very strange. As if he'd been deliberately concealing it. And you had no idea that he might have some ESP talent working for him?"

Jeff scowled. "Not even a hint. I hadn't even thought of it, until I found that card. Then hindsight started reminding me of funny things I hadn't noticed before."

Harpo grunted. "Yes. I suppose that's how it would be. But Schiml must have had direct evidence. This ESP study is just like space warp rocket engines were before they found the Koenig drive: lots of people were sure it could be done, lots of attempts every time a new angle turned up, but they just didn't know how to do it. Then Koenig came up with his space curvature equations, turned Einstein's work upside down, and from then on it was as easy as falling off a log." The big man paused, flushed apologetically. "I was a Koenig drive engineer once, before I got the virus and ended up too slow to hang on," he explained. "But never mind."

"Well, it's true," Jacques interrupted, "Schiml must

have known. And now he's ready to dump us out on the street, after all the work we've done. If somebody opens the door to ESP around here, there won't be any other kind of work in the Center for twenty years. And if we don't happen to be able to fit in—" He ran his finger across his throat, scowling. "The man is here. We know who he is. Now we need information on him, past and present. That means we'll have to search the archives. There's no other way." He looked at Jeff. "You know how the files work. You're the one who can dig what we need to know out of the archives."

Jeff nodded. "But I'll need time there to work without interruption. Can you get me into the archive files without being caught?"

"Nothing to it. Give us half an hour to take care of the guards and clear the way. The old fire alarm gag should do it. Right, Harpo? Then Jeff can walk right down there."

"And can you keep it clear for me for an hour at least?" Jeff said.

"Take five hours if you need it. We'll keep it clear." Harpo stood up sharply. "Let's go, Jacques. Wait for thirty minutes, then come down. I'll set the wrist alarm here on the table. Blackie, you draw him a map while he waits." The bald-headed giant started to leave, then turned back. "And don't worry if you hear some ruckus outside. This isn't the first time we've had to keep the guards running in circles." He touched his forehead in a sort of salute; then he and the Nasty Frenchman disappeared into the corridor.

## VI

"I THINK IT might work." Jeff breathed, tucking Blackie's crude penciled map into his pocket. "I think maybe we've got him. Once we know where he is, and what they're planning to do with him and where—" He grinned up at her. "His number's coming up, Blackie. It was bound to, sooner or later."

The girl leaned forward, pouring coffee, sitting silently. Jeff studied her face as if seeing it for the first time. Somehow it seemed softer now than before; in the dim light of the room the hard lines melted away as if by magic and she looked younger and fresher than he remembered. But she had been silent as the plans were made, and now her eyes were vaguely troubled as she lifted her coffee cup in mock salute. "To the hunter," she said softly.

Jeff nodded. "Thanks. But not for long, now."

"It better not be for long," she said. "Becuase your number's up too."

"You mean for assignment?" He laughed. "I know it. But that's the way it is. I'm following this through to the end, now, no matter what happens."

"Jeff, you *can't* sign a release."

Jeff stared at her in the silent room. "But that's where you're wrong," he said softly. "I don't *want* to, no. But if I have to, if the chips are really down, I will."

Her eyes were wide and very dark. "Jeff, listen to me! You're in terrible danger here."

"I know that."

"No, you don't. You really don't." The girl was shaking her head, tears coming to her eyes. "You don't know anything, Jeff, about the Mercy Men, or the things they do. Oh, I know you think you know, but you *don't*, really. Look, Jeff, think straight instead of crazy for a minute. You're young, you're smart, there are other ways to spend your life, more important things for you to do. Can't you see that? This Conroe isn't worth risking your life for, no matter *what* he's done to you or to your father. And that's what you're doing here. You're walking into a death trap! *Get out*, while you can."

Jeff shook his head doggedly. "I can't get out. I just can't. Nothing anyone could say could drive me out now. I just need a little time."

"But you haven't *got* time! Fine, go down there tonight if you have to, *try* to find him, but if you don't find him fast, then cut and run! Get out, *tonight*. They can't stop you *yet*, they have no legal hold on you, *yet*. But once you sign a release, they've got you. *It'll be too late to run then.*"

Jeff sat down on the bed, looking at the girl. There was an elfin expression on her face, a curious intensity in her large gray eyes that he had never seen before. "What do you care?" he asked suddenly. "What do you care *what* I do?"

Her voice was low, and the words tumbled out so fast that he could hardly follow them. "Look, Jeff, you and me, we could work as a team. Between the two of us, with the dice, we've got something big. Don't you see what we could do? We could get out of here, together we could get out of the city, go to the West Coast. The dice, think of the dice, man! We could clean up! You don't belong here, hung up on the rack for slaughter. And I don't belong here, either, if we could work together."

Somewhere in the distance an alarm bell began ringing, insistently, clang-clanging down the corridors. They heard a rush of feet past the door, shouted orders, the shrill of a guard's whistle. Three jitneys went by in rapid succession. Abruptly, the corridor fell silent again. But

Jeff hardly noticed the hubbub. He was staring at the girl. "Blackie, Blackie, think what you're saying. The tough-luck jinx—have you forgotten? You're safe from it here. But outside, what would happen? We might make a go of it, sure, but suppose not? Suppose the jinx followed us?"

"I just don't think it would." She swallowed as she tried to blink back tears. "Maybe it sounds silly, but it isn't just selfishness, Jeff. I could stay here. I talked to Schiml this afternoon, before Harpo and Jacques even heard about the new man. Jacques is right. They're out, if ESP work turns up. But I'm not. Schiml wants me to stay, he says they've got a job for me, but I don't *want* to stay. I don't want you to stay either."

Jeff sat silent for a moment. Suddenly he was very tired, and confused. "It's no good, Blackie," he said at last. "Not yet, not now. After I find Conroe, after I get out, then maybe. I haven't even thought about this dice business, it hasn't mattered enough. Because I've got something else I have to do."

"Then do it, but *fast*. Find this man tonight. Then get out, before something terrible happens."

On the table the wrist alarm began buzzing insistently. Jeff reached out, snapped it off. Their eyes met. "Don't worry," he said gently. "Nothing's going to happen. I've been at this too long for anything to happen now."

There was something in her face as she looked up at him, a depth and sincerity that wasn't there before. "You stubborn knot-head. You just don't know." She touched his cheek and kissed him, and then they clung to each other for a moment, and he heard her voice at his ear. "Jeff—"

He put a finger to his lips, loosened her arms from him gently. "Don't say it, Blackie. Not now." They clung for a moment more, and then he was outside, moving down the corridor, feeling the cool air on his cheek. At the down stairway he began to run, eager not to lose a moment the others had prepared for him. He knew the end of the trail was near.

## VII

JACQUES AND Harpo were waiting for him at the foot of the escalator. He nodded to them and followed them down the corridor to the small jitney car that was waiting. "Everything set?"

"Yes. The guards are all busy in the 12-B unit putting out a fire. I don't think they'll be back for a couple of hours." The Nasty Frenchman scowled. "But you'll have to hurry. When they do come back, we might have trouble stalling them again."

Jeff nodded. "That should be enough time. Then maybe we'll have some other things to keep the guards busy tonight."

They climbed into the jitney. Harpo took the controls, running the little car swiftly down the corridor. It swung suddenly into a pitch-black tunnel, took a nose dive and began to spiral swiftly downward. Jeff grabbed onto the handrail, gasping. "What's wrong?"

Harpo chuckled. "Nothing. It's just a long way down. Remember, the archives hold the permanent records of the entire Hoffman Center since it was first opened. That's why they're in a vault. Even pinpoint bombing couldn't destroy those records."

Presently the jitney leveled out and swung into a lighted corridor. Jeff swallowed, and felt his ears pop. For another five minutes the car moved along through a maze of tunnels and corridors; finally it reached a dead end before a steel vault door and settled down to the floor.

Without a word Harpo moved down to the open end of the corridor, drawing the jitney car behind him. He opened the motor hood, started pawing around busily inside. The Nasty Frenchman chuckled. "If anyone wanders by, that jitney traffic horn goes off, and Harpo's just a poor technician trying to make it stop." The little man walked quickly to the steel door.

"You think you're going to get in there?" Jeff asked, pointing to the vault.

"It won't be the first time I've sprung one of those," Jacques retorted. "This one I know inside and out. A few months ago we wanted in there, when they were trying to pull some kind of a shakedown deal on some of us. I worked out the combination pattern; it took me three days. Of course they change the combination every month or so, but the pattern is always the same." He opened a small leather kit, placed an instrument up against the lock, and stood poised with a long thin wire ready in his other hand. Jeff heard several muffled clicks; then Jacques inserted the wire sharply into something. An alarm bell above the door gave one dull, half-hearted clunk and relapsed into silence, as if it had decided at the last moment that it didn't really want to ring after all. A few moments later Jacques looked up and winked at Jeff.

Slowly, the vault door swung open.

The place smelled damp and empty. Three walls and half the fourth were occupied with electronic file controls. The bulk of the room was taken up with tables, microviewers, readers, recorders, and other study apparatus. There was nothing small in the room; the whole place breathed of bigness, of complexity, of many years of work and wisdom. Many lives were recorded in this room, and many, many deaths. Something suggested that it was built to hold the records of many more.

Jeff moved toward the central control panel, located the master coder, and sat down before it. He examined it carefully, as though sizing up what this mammoth filing machine could reveal to him and what it might do. Suddenly he was afraid. A face was looming up in his mind, a familiar face that had come to him again and again in his dreams. It was a hateful, almost inhuman face—but was that all? Or was there more to that face, more to those nightmares, than he had ever suspected? Something stirred deep in his mind, and his hand trembled as he reached out to touch the control panel. A ghost was there at his elbow, a phantom that had followed him on a long, bitter trail. And now that the end of the trail might be right here in this room, he was afraid.

He shook his head, angry at himself. This was no time for panic. This was not a nightmare now, this was real. He found the master code panels and punched the code for the Mercy Men, research unit. Then he computed the coding for Conroe's name. With trembling fingers he typed out the coding, punched the tracer button, and sat back, waiting for the tell-tale file cards and folio to drop into the slot.

The file buzzed and chattered and whirred and moaned, and finally the read-out panel lighted up: NO INFORMATION.

Jeff blinked, incredulous. These files were the final appeal; the information *had* to be here. Quickly he computed a description coding, fed it in, and waited again. Still no information. He picked up the code card from his pocket, the card he had stolen from the Mercy Men's file, with the Hoffman Center's own mug shot of Conroe on it, and fed it into the photoelectric tracer. He threw the switch for an unlimited file search, coded the special instructions: "Any person resembling this description in any way; any information." Again he sat back, breathing heavily.

The whirring went on and on. Then, inexorably, the read-out panel spelled out a single word: "UNKNOWN."

It was no longer just merely odd; it was downright impossible. Jeff went through the whole coding process again, step by step, certain he had made an error. There wasn't any error—and yet, the files were empty of information. As though there had never been a Paul Conroe. There was not even a reference to the card in the Mercy Men's files, here in the one place where there *had* to be complete information.

It was dead end. There wasn't any other place to go.

Behind him the Nasty Frenchman stirred, lit a cigarette. "What's the matter, no luck?"

"No luck," Jeff said. "We're whipped. That's all."

"But there must be *some* information about him."

"*Well, there's not!*" Jeff slammed his fist down on the desk with a crash. "There's not a trace, not a whisper of the man. There *has* to be, but there's not. It's the same as every other time: a blank wall. And there have been too many blank walls. I'm getting tired of always running into blank walls." He stood up, his shoulders sagging. "I'm too tired to keep it up. There's no point to playing this game any more. I'm getting out of here while there's still time."

Jacques eyed him in alarm. "Maybe you've got more time than you think," he said hastily. "This is no time to be running out. It could be weeks before you were assigned."

Jeff stared at him. "Well, I know a way to find *that* out, at least." He walked over to the control panel, stabbed an angry finger at the master coder, picked out the coding for J. K. Meyer. "If these are really the master files they'll have me in here, won't they? Everything they know about me: what the testing said, what they're planning to do to me, and when. So let's just look and see how much time I've got." Quickly he punched out the coding, and pushed the tracer button.

The machinery whirred again, briefly. There was a click in the receiver slot, and another, and another. Jeff blinked at it as the microfilm rolls continued to fall down. Then he reached out for the single white card which had fallen down on top of the microfilm. He picked it up gingerly. His own death warrant, perhaps? Hard to say, but maybe he'd better know. He looked at the card, and froze.

"J. K. Meyer" he had punched in, and that was what the card said—*but not Jeffrey K. Meyer.* The card bore a photo of a middle-aged, gray-haired man, and the typewritten name at the top said: JACOB K. MEYER.

*The picture was a photo of his father's face.*

## VIII

IN THESE past three years, Jeff Meyer thought, he had hardened himself beyond vulnerability. Certainly he had learned to believe things he once would have thought unbelievable. But this was incredible in every possible degree.

He stared at the card in his hand, expecting it to vanish, but it did not go away. It remained in his hands, and the name "Jacob K. Meyer" was still written across the top. The picture still showed the features he knew were those of his father, staring up at him mutely from the card.

*His father!* Jeff groped for the chair, his heart pounding. Below the name and picture was a typewritten notation: "Born 11 August 2030, Des Moines, Iowa; married 3 December 2077 to Greta Towne Schuler; wife died hepatitis 27 November 2082; one son Jeffrey born 16 September 2078." Below this were a series of dates: date of Bachelor's degree, date of Master's and Doctorate; Associate Professor of probability theory and statistics at the University of the East, 2079-2084; joined the government in the Department of Statistics in 2085; died 14 March 2087; cause of death classified, see references. Finally, at the bottom of the card, a long series of code numbers referring to microfilm files.

Jeff stared at the numbers . . . dozens of numbers . . . with his mind spinning. Finally he looked up at the Nasty Frenchman, "You might as well go," he said. "I've got some reading to do." Eagerly he scooped up the microfilm rolls and carried them to the nearest reader. He twisted a spool into the machine, and threw on the light switch.

The first roll was a long, detailed series of abstracts of statistical papers all written by Jacob K. Meyer, Ph.D., all covered with marginal notes in a scrawling, spidery hand and initialled "R.D.S." The papers covered a multitude of statistical studies: population densities, space-tenant ratios, traffic flow-patterns, stock market fluctuations—anything and everything, or so it seemed. Some apparently dealt with the very techniques of statistical analysis. Others were concerned with specific places those techniques had been applied.

The papers were written in a scholarly manner, well documented, precise and reasonable, but the marginal notes seemed to disagree, criticizing continually both the samplings used in the studies and the conclusions that had been drawn. Jeff read through some of the papers, scowling; they dated over the period of four years when his father had been teaching statistics at the university. There were several dozen papers in all, each one bearing the marginal notes. None of them made much sense to Jeff. With a sigh he rewound the roll and fed in another.

This one was different. It was a correspondence file with a multitude of letters written by, to, or about Jeff's father. One caught Jeff's eye: a letter dated almost twenty years before, addressed to the Government Bureau of Standards and signed by Roger D. Schiml, M.D. Jeff skimmed it, then paused to read more closely: "—as director of research at the Hoffman Medical Research Center, I considered it my duty to bring this unbelievable condition to your attention. Naturally, a statistical analysis will have to be made before we can conclude that there has been a real and significant increase in the percentage of incidence of mental illness in the country, but we believe the evidence is very suggestive. We have followed Dr. Meyer's work in statistical analysis with much interest in the past and would be pleased if he could arrange to come to the Hoffman Center within the next month to commence such a study for us. . . ." Still nothing very exciting, except that it explained why Jacob Meyer had a file at the Hoffman Center at all. Or did it? If the "R.D.S." of the marginal notes meant Roger D. Schiml, then he seemed to disagree with practically everything Jacob Meyer had ever written about statistics. Why, then, would he be asking to hire the man to do a statistical analysis for the Hoffman Center? Jeff puzzled a moment, then went on to more correspondence. Another letter came up, written by some unidentified individual and directed to Dr. Schiml, dated almost a year later than the former letter. This note referred several times to the "almost unbelievable results of the statistical study reported several months ago," and also referred to an investigation just concluded of possible disturbing elements in the analysis. The final paragraph of the letter Jeff read through three times:

"There can be no doubt that the data Dr. Meyer used was sound, and properly collected. Naturally, the results he then reported followed mathematically from the data and should have been valid. When our own studies proved that those results were, in fact, wildly *invalid,* we knew that the source of the trouble had to lie in some totally unsuspected disturbing or distorting factor.

"Reluctant as we are to bring this matter to your attention, we are forced to the unbelievable conclusion that in some fashion or another Dr. Jacob K. Meyer *was himself* the sole disturbing factor in the analysis.

How this could be possible we do not know, but no other conclusion fits the facts. We therefore urge that you undertake an intensive study of Dr. Meyer's previous work to see if such aberrant results have occurred before, and if so, when and how. We also recommend that this be done without delay. Meanwhile, we must all assume that Dr. Meyer is a very sick . . . and possibly very dangerous . . . man, and take appropriate action to protect others as well as himself."

At the top of the letter, and again under the signature, were stamped the government's careful restrction in red letters: TOP SECRET.

Another letter appeared on the reader screen. This bore the letterhead of a New York psychiatrist. Jeff read it through in horrified fascination:

Dear Dr. Schiml:

We have studied the microfilm records you sent us with extreme care, and have undertaken a psychiatric analysis of Dr. Jacob K. Meyer from his work, as you requested. Although a final diagnosis must await interviewing and examination of the patient in person, we are inclined to support your suspicions. There is little doubt that this man is gravely unbalanced. As to the possibility of his mental illness being in some way connected with various remarkable extrasensory phenomena, we cannot say; psychiatric authorities, as you know, have never been convinced that ESP actually exists at all. But we must point out that this man almost certainly undergoes a regular manic-depressive cycle of psychosis. He may be dangerously depressed, even suicidal, in a depressive low, and could well endanger himself and others during a period of wild elation. Such a person is extremely dangerous, and should certainly be confined for treatment.

Jeff read the letter a second time, trembling with anger. What lies! The idea that his father might have been insane, that he could ever have falsified any sort of statistical report that he had done—it was impossible, a pack of incredible lies. Yet those lies were here in the files of the greatest medical center on the face of the earth. Lies about his father, lies that Jeff couldn't even attack because he could not understand them.

The door swung open sharply and the Nasty Frenchman stuck his head in, panting. He obviously had been running. "You've got to get out of here," he said. "Something's wrong, a whole squad of guards are coming down." He disappeared abruptly and Jeff heard Harpo's bass voice bellow at him, "Come on, *move!* We've got to run!"

Jeff's legs would hardly move. He felt numb when he scrambled to his feet as though a thousand nerve centers had suddenly been jolted at once. His hands were clumsy as he stuffed the microfilm rolls into his pockets. There was no sense to what he had just seen, it made no sense whatever. Somehow, he knew, there must be some tie-in between these letters about his father, written so long ago, and the absence of any information on Paul Conroe in the files. But he couldn't find the link. He ran out the vault door. Harpo and Jacques were holding the jitney car for him. The moment he leaped in, the car took off down a dark tunnel and began the long spiral ascent to the upper levels At the same time, Jeff heard the loud, insistent clang of alarm bells both above them and below.

Harpo braked the car sharply. "Oh, oh," he said softly. "They're onto us, all right—that's a general muster. If we really run for it, we may get back to quarters before they nail us, but if we get stopped, it's every man for himself."

The Nasty Frenchman nodded, and Harpo made the car leap forward. As they came out into a lighted corridor, Jeff saw the results of the alarm: not a soul was in sight. Somewhere, he realized, a tracer board would have spotted a moving car. But if they could disembark and send the car on—

They sped along as minutes dragged. At last he saw the familiar escalator ahead. All three jumped out as the car moved past and on down a tunnel; moments later they were running pell-mell up to the corridor of 17-D.

Even as they ran, Jeff could not forget the letters he had read. All the way up from the vault, uneasy thoughts kept flooding his mind. Things began falling into place. Things he had overlooked, or ignored, or forgotten began to fit together—not to form answers, but to form *questions*.

Big questions which could no longer be evaded. Like the question of Paul Conroe, for instance. It was far too pat and easy that Conroe should come to this place and then vanish as if he had never been alive. Things wouldn't happen that way, even for Conroe, unless he knew where he was coming when he came here. Other things came into focus, too: things that had happened years before, things that seemed to swim up out of his memory and then, just as he was about to get hold of them, would duck back out of reach again. Things like that strange evening here in the game room . . . or like the episode in the nightclub with the girl who looked like Blackie but wasn't. Things like the sudden, shocking jolt that had pulled him out of deep hypnosis in the testing room and driven him, wild with terror, face first into a brick wall. Things like the letters he had seen in the vault.

*What did these things mean?*

Whatever they meant, he was afraid. As he reached the top of the escalator on Harpo's heels he broke into a run down the corridor toward his room, suddenly and unreasoningly afraid. He tore open the door, fell inside and slammed it behind him before snapping on the lights.

He knew then, very clearly, that he had to get out. Not later. *Now,* while he could still run. Without any reason or proof he suddenly knew that he would never find Paul Conroe here, not the way he had thought he would. He would never find Conroe in a million years. And he knew, very clearly, why.

Because in all these three years it had not been Jeff hunting Conroe; *it had been Conroe hunting Jeff.* He had not driven Conroe here; *Conroe had lured him here.* He was not here because Conroe was trying to escape from him; he was here because *Dr. Schiml had wanted Jeff Meyer here as a Mercy Man.* Nothing more.

Jacob Meyer's son. . . .

Moving swiftly, Jeff tore open his foot locker, stared at the empty hooks. The locker had been cleaned out. His bag was gone, his shoes were gone, his clothes were gone.

He whirled around in panic. The escalator! If he could get to the bottom and into a corridor, he might find a jitney. At least he could be moving, then, searching the way up to the ground level. He peeked out into the empty hall, then ran for the escalator. When he was halfway there, a wire cage slammed down across the corridor, blocking his path completely.

Jeff stopped short, his shoes scraping against the concrete floor. He stared, uncomprehending, at the wire grill; then he whirled and ran back along the corridor as fast as he could move. At the next turn, before the game room, he had seen a side passage leading to a Y. If he could reach that, perhaps. . . .

Another grill clanged down ten yards ahead, and he saw he was trapped. Caged up tight in one hundred-yard length of corridor. He clutched at the wire, and suddenly he thought of Blackie. She had been gone. Where to? Where had everybody gone? Could this all have been some kind of fantastic trap involving Blackie and Jacques, even Harpo? He turned back, frantically jerking doors open, staring into room after room.

All empty.

So it *was* a trap. Except that *he* was the quarry, not Conroe.

Suddenly his fear seemed to vanish, and he was very calm. He saw a pattern as he looked into room after room, all empty, and felt a curious sense of inevitability. All right, it was a trap. Nobody else was here, and he wasn't going anywhere. He reached his own room again, walked in leaving the door wide open and sat down on the bed with a sigh.

He didn't have to wait very long. A moment later there was a clank of grillwork being unlocked, and the sound of feet in the corridor. Then Dr. Schiml was standing in the door, still in his surgeon's cap and gown, flanked by gray-clad guards. He walked into the room and sank down on the bed opposite with an audible sigh. Blackie followed him. Her eyes were downcast, avoiding Jeff's. She was tossing a little pair of ivory dice into the air, catching them as they fell.

The doctor smiled and drew a crisp white paper from his pocket, began unfolding it slowly. "A matter of business," he said, almost apologetically. "It's time that we got down to business, I think. Don't you?"

IX

JEFF MEYER looked up at the doctor's face. His throat felt like sandpaper. He tried to swallow, and couldn't. "Sorry," he said. "I've changed my mind. I'm not talking business."

Dr. Schiml chuckled and shook his head slowly back and forth. "I'm afraid you are. I hear you're quite handy at the dice, isn't that right?"

Jeff jumped out of the chair, fists clenched, eyes

blazing at the girl. "So it *was* you," he snarled. "You'd sell your grandmother short for a bag of salt, wouldn't you? Come to me with your sob stories, beg me to move out of here with you." His voice was bitter. "How much did they pay you to sell out? A hundred thousand, maybe? Or was this just sort of a routine job? Maybe a thousand or two?"

The girl's face darkened. "No, that's not true. I didn't—"

"Well, it won't do them any good anyway, and you aren't likely to get paid, either. Because I'm not signing any release, now or ever."

A guard took Jeff's arm, crowded him back down into the chair. Dr. Schiml was still smiling, clasping his knee with his hands. "I guess you didn't quite understand me," he said pleasantly. "You mustn't blame Blackie. She didn't sell you short. She just couldn't help answering a few perfectly innocent questions." His eyes turned to Jeff, cold. "We're not asking you to sign a release, Jeff. We're telling you."

"Don't be silly," Jeff said. "I don't care what you tell me. I won't sign a release for you people for anything. Do you think I've lost my mind?" He snatched up the release form, looked at it, and tore it into shreds. "Here's your release. Now go burn it, and then get yourself some other guinea pig."

"But we don't *want* some other guinea pig," Schiml said quietly. "That's just it, you see. We want *you*, Jeff."

Jeff felt sweat on his forehead. "Look, I'm not signing *anything*, don't you understand? I've changed my mind. I don't care for the work here, I don't like the company."

Schiml shrugged. "Sorry you tore that up," he said, pulling out another sheet of paper. "But it doesn't really matter. Here's the photostat of the one we have up in my vault. The one you signed under hypnosis during the testing." He looked up at the guards. "Bring him along, boys."

"Wait!" Jeff was on his feet again, facing the guards

like a trapped animal. His eyes caught Schiml's. "Look, you've got things wrong. I'm a fake in here, a fraud. Can't you understand that? I didn't come to volunteer. I never intended to volunteer, never planned to go even as far as I did. I came here—"

Schiml cut him off impatiently. "Yes, yes, I know all that. You came into this place because you followed a man, a man you've been trying to nail down for years because you think he murdered your father and nothing would do but you find out why. Right?" Schiml blinked down at Jeff. "All right, that was your choice. You came in here, and went through testing, hunting down your man, trying to find him right under our noses. Did you think we didn't know? But you didn't find him, and now all of a sudden things are a little too hot for you, so you've decided that it's time to pull out, right? Or have we got some of the details wrong?"

Jeff's jaw went slack as he listened. "That rotten girl. . . ."

Schiml grimaced. "Don't blame Blackie, she didn't squeal. In fact, Blackie is very discreet, in her own way. She hasn't had anything to do with it, Jeff. We've known all about you right along, from a much closer source than Blackie." He glanced over his shoulder at one of the guards. "Bring him in," he said abruptly.

The door of the adjoining room opened, and a man walked in. He was a tall, lean man; gaunt-faced man with sallow cheeks and large, sad eyes; a weary-looking man whose hair was graying at the temples, a man who looked desperately tired.

Schiml looked at the man, and then looked at the ceiling. "Hello, Paul," he said softly. "There's a man here who's been looking for you."

Jeff stared at the man and screamed—an animal cry of rage that echoed in the room. He twisted free of the guards who were holding his arms and lunged at Paul Conroe. It was not willful, this explosion of hatred in his mind, but it was there; it had been there all the time. Conroe leaped back with a cry, and Schiml was on his feet. "Get out of here, Paul, quick!" he cried as the guards grappled Jeff's arms again.

But Conroe did not move. He was standing writhing, his hands clamped to his head, helpless to move as Jeff glared at him. And then, incredibly, the coffee cup rose from the table of its own accord and whirled through the air straight for Conroe's head. It missed and smashed against the wall. The other cup followed— *smash!*—and then the pot—*crash!* Jeff cried out again, and the plaster began peeling off the walls and ceiling in great chunks that crumbled to the floor. The table pitched over and a chair hurtled through the air. The curtains suddenly started to blaze, as if ignited by some magic fire. An instant later, Conroe's own clothing began to smoke and smolder. . . .

Blackie screamed, staring at Jeff in open horror. Schiml's voice roared through the bedlam. *"Get him! Stun him out before he tears the place down around our ears!"* Again Jeff cried out mindlessly, and this time it was Conroe shouting: "Stop him—he's tearing me apart inside. Please, somebody, stop him!"

Someone stepped between Jeff and Conroe. There was a flash of a stun-gun, and suddenly Jeff's muscles gave out. Like a small, controlled lightning bolt the charge struck, painlessly, almost gently, and he felt himself sliding to the floor. His last conscious impression was of Blackie, standing in the corner with her face in her hands, sobbing like a child.

## Part Four

# THE MERCY MEN

## I

To Jeff Meyer it seemed like a dream. He lay on the long table, wrapped in cool green surgical linens, motionless, barely breathing. His eyes were wide open; he could see the glowing overhead light in the ceiling, hear sounds around him, identify faces, but all feeling was gone. He seemed to be in some strange world where no human foot had ever trod.

Gradually, his awareness increased. He could hear the harsh sound of his own breathing, sometimes slowing almost to a stop, sometimes quickening. Occasionally he could sense rather than see Dr. Schiml pause at his side, stand motionless waiting for a moment, then move on. Jeff himself had no desire to move. He lay like a corpse, but he was not a corpse; across the room he could see the panel of lights flickering on and off, brighter and dimmer, proof that he was alive, if he needed proof. Jeff was not a neuro-physiologist, but he understood the meaning of those flickering lights. The lights were simply reflecting, in simple on-off patterns, the myriads of signals arising from his own mind at that very moment, transmitted to the machine from the microscopic electrodes gently and delicately placed in contact with the key centers of his brain. The micro-surgery necessary must already have been done, but he was not afraid. The techniques had been perfected long since by Hoffman Center surgeons; no harm was done.

But reading and interpreting the signals was something else. No human being could ever hope to analyze the waxing and waning of the flickering light patterns on that panel, not even in a dozen lifetimes, but an electronic camera grid could pick up those changes, instant after instant, flickering and flashing and glowing on and off, in a thousand thousand kaleidoscopic patterns. A computer could fix those changes in its memory banks, sequences of twisted molecules and endlessly reverberating circuits, and then analyze them, and compare them, and integrate them into the constantly changing image visible on the small screen by the bedside. The screen images were not the accurate images passing through Jeff's mind, much was lost in translation, but enough remained to be used. This whole electronic complex was a crude instrument with which to probe the output of such an exquisitely delicate and variable instrument as a human brain, and no one could know this more painfully than Roger Schiml, but even such a crude instrument, Jeff knew, was enough to let Schiml at least observe the strange half-world of another man's mind.

*Then why aren't you afraid, Jeff?* He had no answer to his own question. Across the room he could see Paul Conroe sitting motionless, his face drawn, his gaunt cheeks sunken like the cheeks of a skeleton. Conroe was watching the picture panel too, and his hands were shaking as he lit his pipe. "It's so dangerous," he said at last, turning to Schiml. "So incredibly dangerous."

Schiml nodded gravely, adjusting the microvernier that controlled the probing instrument. "Of course it's dangerous," he acknowledged, exactly as if Jeff were nowhere near. "It probably always will be, but not nearly so dangerous as it would have been twenty years ago. We wouldn't have dared even to try a full-depth mind probe in those days; just placing the electrodes might have been fatal. But we haven't been wasting our time all these years we've been waiting for this man. We've been improving techniques, ironing out bugs. He'll survive, all right, unless we run into something totally unexpected."

Conroe was shaking his head. "I didn't mean just dangerous for *him*. I meant dangerous for *us*. Even he doesn't realize what he can do with that mind of his. How are *we* supposed to guess?" He looked up at Schiml, his eyes fearful. "That room down there—it would have been *gone* in another five minutes if you hadn't stunned him. He'd have torn it apart into molecular dust; it looks as if a wrecking crew had been in there, as it is. Yet I'd swear he didn't know what he was doing. I'm not dead sure he even knew what was *happening*. But wreck the place he did. And that fire was real fire, Roger. I know. I felt it burn me."

Schiml was nodding his head. "Of course it was real fire! Set molecules to spinning at terrifically accelerated rates, and you have fire. We didn't know he could do it; now we do. But those are the things we have to learn, Paul: what this man can do."

Motionless, listening, Jeff heard the words, first uncomprehending, then horrified by his dawning realization. *That's you they're talking about, Jeff. You. You were doing things with molecules that you did with dice in the game room. And it is you, not just anyone, that Schiml has been waiting for all these years.*

Conroe was talking again. "Of course we could both see the fire, but there was something even worse that I think you missed completely. You couldn't feel the blind hatred in that room. I *could* feel it." He looked up. "Roger, how could a man hate that way and not even know it? It was thick as syrup, that hatred. Oh, I've encountered anger before in the minds I've contacted, a thousand times, but never anything like *that*." Conroe sighed. "Well, it's there in his mind, Roger. Seeing me triggered it, and he almost killed me. I'd hate to think what may happen if we probe the right places and trigger the same thing or worse. But knowing it's there in his mind doesn't help. We've got to know *why*."

Schiml nodded again. "That's the key question, of course. *Why does he hate you so much?* When we know that, we may have the answer to twenty years of work." Schiml spread his hands. "Dangerous as it is, we've got to find out, while we have a chance. You know that, Paul. We can't stop now, not with what we already know. We know that Jeff's insanity is far less active, so far, than his father's was. But unless we can find the location in his mind of *both* factors, the psychosis and the extrasensory power, we're lost. We'd have no choice but to turn the whole thing over to the government. And you know what that would mean."

Conroe nodded wearily. "Yes, I know. Riots, slaughter, witch hunts, fear, panic—all the wrong answers. With the insanity that is already abroad, just the panic alone would be fatal."

Dr. Schiml shrugged and came back to the bedside. Jeff could see the man's face clearly above him, with its lines of tension and weariness. Strangely, there was compassion there too, the first time Jeff had noticed. "Well, we'll know very soon," Schiml was saying. "The deep signals are beginning to come through." Jeff heard the words and felt a tingling deep in his mind. And now, suddenly, coldly, he was *really* afraid.

## II

*The needle moved, probed, ever so slightly, stimulating deep, deep in the soft, fragile tissue . . . seeking, probing, recording. A twinge, the barest trace of shock, a sharp series of nerve cells firing in sequence, a flicker of light, a picture—Jeff Meyer shifted, his eyelids droop-*

*ing very slightly. A muscle in his jaw began to twitch. . . .*

He was floating gently, on his back, resting on huge, fluffy, billowing clouds. He didn't know where he was, nor did he care. He just lay there, spinning lazily like a man in free fall, feeling the gentle clouds around him, pressing him downward and downward. His eyes were closed tightly, so tightly that no ray of light might leak in. He knew as he floated that whatever happened he must not open them.

But then there were sounds around him. He felt his muscles tighten as he crossed his arms on his chest and squeezed. There were *things* floating through the air around him, and they were making little sounds, tiny squeaks and groans. He shuddered as the sounds grew louder and turned into voices whispering in his ear, laughing at him.

He opened his eyes wide. He still saw the room, but superimposed was a long, black hollow tunnel he was falling through. He was spinning end over end down the tunnel; he strained to see to the bottom, but he couldn't. Then the laughter started. First a quiet tittering, right beside his ear, but growing louder and louder into chuckles, unpleasant laughter, guffaws. Peal after peal of insane laughter reverberated from the tunnel walls, louder and more derisive by the second. They were *laughing at him*, whoever they were, and their laughs rose to screams in his ears. To escape them he was forced to scream out himself, clasping his hands to his ears, and closing his eyes tightly again.

Abruptly the laughter stopped.

*Everything* stopped.

He lay tense, listening. No, not quite everything. There were *some* sounds, gentle and familiar. Somewhere in the distance he could hear the bzz-bzz-bzz of a cicada. The sound was sharp in the summer night air. Jeff rolled over, felt the clean sheets under him, the soft pillow, the rustling of the light blanket. Where . . . ?

Of course. He was in his room, waiting. Waiting and expecting.

Daddy! Suddenly, he knew that his father had come home. Not from any sound in the dark house, he hadn't even heard the jet car go into the garage, nor the front door squeak, but he knew his father was here, just the same. He blinked at the darkness, a little frightened now that Daddy was here and he could *be* frightened. It was dark in the room, and he didn't *like* the darkness and he wished his father would come up and turn on the light. But ever since Mommy had died Daddy had told him that he had to be a brave little man, even if he was only four, so of course he wasn't frightened when Daddy was gone. . . .

He lay and shivered. There were other noises, outside the window, in the room. Frightening noises. It was all very well to be a brave little man, but Daddy just didn't understand about the dark and the noises, or how badly he wanted somebody to hold him close sometimes and whisper to him, like Mommy used to do. Of course, Mommy had been different. He'd never been able to *feel* Mommy inside his head, the way he could feel his father . . . but Mommy had understood about the dark.

And then he heard his father's step on the stair, and felt him coming nearer. He rolled over, laughing to himself, pretending to be asleep. Not that he'd fool his father for a minute, Daddy already knew he was awake, but they played this same game night after night. It was fun to play little games like that with Daddy. He waited until he heard the door open, and the footsteps reached his bed. Then he rolled over and threw the covers off, and jumped up in bed like a ghost. . . . "Did I scare you?"

After that his father took him up on his shoulders, and laughed, and said he was a big white horse come to carry Jeff on a long journey. So they took a long journey down the stairs to the study for milk and cookies, just as they always did when Daddy came home. He knew his father didn't really want any milk . . . he was much more interested in watching his son play with the funny cards, the cards Jeff had watched him make, a long time ago. They had a game with the cards: his father would look at them, one by one, and Jeff would call out the symbol as soon as he picked it up from his father's mind . . . the circle, the spiral, the figure eight, the letter B, the letter R . . . *it was a letter R, wasn't it, Daddy? But it couldn't have been, I saw a letter B . . . oh, I see you're trying to catch me! Can we play with the marbles now? Or the dice? Let's use the round-cornered ones, they're easier, you know.*

His father would watch him as he read off the cards, wrinkling up his nose and calling out the symbols. He would see his father mark down each right one and each wrong one; he could tell which was which, every time—and he would *feel* his father's satisfaction and approval. Then the dice would come out, much more fun than the cards. *The squre-cornered dice, daddy? But they're hard to work . . . oh, I see, another game, a new one! Show me how. I'll try very hard to make them come out right.*

And then, after the new game his father told him a story before bed, one of the funny stories where he said all the ordinary words out loud, but put in all the fun and jokes and private things without using any words at all.

It was funny, none of the others like Mary-Ann down the block could feel their fathers the way he could. He wondered about that. Once he had told Mary-Ann about it as a special secret, and she didn't even believe him. *Nobody* can hear their father's words without their fathers talking, she said. But he knew better. Usually it was fun, too, but tonight after the story, and going up to bed, he felt other things from his father's mind . . . things that frightened him. When his father turned off the light to go, Jeff clung to him in the moonlight flooding his bedroom. "Daddy?"

"Yes, son."

"Why . . . why are you afraid, tonight? You're afraid about something, I can tell."

His father laughed and looked at him in a strange way, and said, "Afraid? Nonsense. What do you mean, afraid?" But the afraidness was still there. Even when his father went down the hall to his study, Jeff could still feel the afraidness.

## III

ABRUPTLY, THEN, the small-boy memory faded and things changed. *Everything* changed. One moment he was four years old and alone in his bed, frightened because his father was frightened. The next moment he was in some fantastic dream place he had never known, swinging around the brink of a vast, dark whirlpool. He felt himself being swung around in the blackness, carried without effort, yet he also seemed to be watching himself from a distance, unable to reach out for help. He knew, somehow, that he was still Jeff Meyer and that the delicate electrodes were still attached, searching his mind. He could actually feel the probe approach a memory, then withdraw, then approach again more certainly. He would feel a sudden twinge of recognition, an almost mechanical shock of awareness and realization of truth as a stimulated memory rose to the surface; then the probe would be gone, finished in that area, moving on to the next. The whirlpool became a tunnel of water rushing about him, whirling him up, up, up, around, then down, with a sickening rush, then up again, as though he were riding a great whirling roller-coaster, but always moving in closer and closer. . . .

*To what?*

He didn't know, but he knew he didn't want to go there. He was fighting the probe, resisting it, blocking it off with all his strength, trying to keep it away. He clenched his fists and fought, gritting his teeth, desperate. Down at the end of that tumultuous whirlpool was a place he did not want to go, something he did not want to see. Whatever it was, was fearful and ugly, something that had been wiped out of his mind long ago. Something that had been scoured out and disposed of. Whatever it was, it was *something he dare not face, ever again.*

He felt himself dip down toward the bottom. A memory flickered, and he screamed. Something lay waiting for him down there, something too hideous to imagine. *Something which could kill him* if the probe ever found it . . . he fought harder, trying to break free of the spiraling whirpool.

Then memory flickered again, and this time stayed. *His father was afraid!* The thought struck as a shocking revelation, tightening his muscles into rigid knots. His father was afraid, so terribly afraid! He could feel the fear in his own mind, chillingly, just as he had always felt his father's thoughts. . . .

He opened his eyes and saw green grass under his head. He was on the shady bank of a creek passing through a meadow. The afternoon sun was high, but willows and cottonwoods hung overhead, sheltering him with their cool shade. A few feet away the brook made a gentle, soothing sound as it passed over a small rapids.

He was completely alone, and half dozing. He watched lazily as a bird flitted from branch to branch overhead. A cool breeze from the meadow touched his cheek. It was a glorious lazy summer day, a day made for eight-year-old boys. . . .

"Dad!" The word broke from him involuntarily and he sat bolt upright, frowning in alarm, his hair tousled.

Some corner of his mind, very remote, was telling him that he was not really eight years old, that this was just memory, but it was vivid. He *felt* eight years old, stared down at an eight-year-old's hands, slightly grubby, and an eight-year-old's jeans patched and repatched at the knees. He felt fear, too, but not his own fear. This came from Dad, unmistakably. Something had happened and his father was afraid, running away from something with the desperation of a hunted animal.

The boy waited and cocked his head as though listening might help. In a moment things came into focus and he was seeing with his father's eyes and feeling with his father's mind as he found himself doing so often these days, even when Dad was a long way away. Right now, through his father's mind he was running down a corridor, fleeing from something, half-mad with fear. Reaching the end of the hall, he peered back over his shoulder, and then wrenched vainly at the door that was there. It wouldn't open, and he collapsed against it, sobbing, with tears of fear and desperation running down his cheeks. Jeff could see the door. He could feel his father gasping for breath, and hear the furious pulse pounding in his father's head. He saw the empty, darkened corridor, and then his mind was swept up in his father's thoughts, the strange, wild, crazy kind of thoughts that flooded his father's mind so often these days . . . the confused scrambled nightmare thoughts that frightened Jeff so much. But right now, far stronger than ever before, his thoughts were his father's thoughts as though their two minds were one, the closest rapport he had ever felt before. And there beside the summer brook Jeff held his hands to his head, writhing with the pain and fear his father was suffering somewhere miles away.

*They're coming*, his mind was crying out. *Trapped, trapped! What can I do?*

He was racing back up the corridor now, back to the elevator standing open. It was the only chance. He ran outside, groped frantically for the switch. He had to get away, had to get down below, somehow get to the street. Up here he was trapped. What a stupid mistake to walk into a place like this office building, of all places. Such an obvious trap, when he *knew* they were closing in on him! Why had he come here, *why?* Of course he knew they were hunting him, getting closer every day, but how could he have foreseen that this day would bring a business panic? How could he have told that on this particular day the stock market would take such a violent plunge that the hunters would *know* that he had to be the cause, and could pinpoint his exact location? It had *never* happened so violently before; how could he have foreseen it? And this was to have been the final test to prove the terrible power that he had, a force that poured from his mind in some incomprehensible, uncontrollable way, more and more violently every day, twisting and altering and destroying everything he came near.

That was why they were hunting him, of course. They knew it wasn't malicious. They *knew* he couldn't control it or prevent it. They also knew that no prison or hospital could hold him, not any longer. And in his rare rational moments he realized they had no choice but to destroy him. . . .

*But not now!* Please, not now, not when he was so close to the answer. Slowly, helpless anger flooded his mind. It wasn't fair. He'd fight them. They had no *right* to stop him now; in another day, another week, he would have the answer. In another few days he would have corralled this frightening power, *controlled* it. He knew he could find out how, he was on the very brink of it already. And now, of all times they had him trapped, and they would not listen to pleas any longer.

*Why, Dad? Why are they hunting you? Oh, please, come home, I'm scared of what's happenings. Please don't be so much afraid, it makes me afraid too. . . .*

The elevator gave a lurch, and he fell against the

door as the car stopped between floors. Frantically he pounded the button, waited through long eternities as the car hung motionless? *What are they doing?* He ran his fingers along the cracks in the car door, seeking a hold, trying to wrench open the locked door. They were close, now, some above him, some below. Something broke in his mind then, some last dam of control gave way and he was screaming his defiance at them, screaming his hatred, his bitterness. They had him trapped. They were going to kill him without trial, shoot him down like a mad dog. He could feel them flinch and draw back at the stream of hatred he was pouring out at them, these hunters who had been tracking him down. With insane glee he felt them cringe. *They were afraid of him,* but they were determined to kill him all the same.

Above him he heard a sound. He flattened back against the elevator wall, tearing at the metal grating to find some escapeway into the shaft below. One of them was coming down from above, onto the top of the elevator; a man who was afraid of him, but who was still moving down with fixed determination. There was a scraping sound from above, a dull twang of cable striking against cable.

*They could be cutting the car loose!* He leaped for the ceiling of the car, reaching up for the little escapeway door. On the third jump he caught the ring latch and pulled the door open. Another leap, and his hand caught the rim of the opening and he was dragging himself up, twisting his shoulders through until he was on top of the car.

He looked up. A man was up above him in the shaft, clinging to the cables twenty feet up. His legs were wrapped around them. In one hand was a gun. He saw the man's face, sallow and gaunt, frightened, with a high forehead and slightly bulging eyes.

Even as he watched, the man inched down another foot. *Shake him off, Dad! Stop him, don't let him kill you!* Jacob Meyer grabbed at the cables, shook them like some kind of steel vine, and he saw the man hold tighter as the cables vibrated, then moved down another foot.

*Stop him!*

The man's face was closer now as he swung on the cable, slowly turning, lifting the weapon, patiently trying to take aim. *Look at him, Jeff! Remember that face, never forget that face! That is the man who is executing your father without a trial.* Hatred poured out at the man. Dad crouched back against the wall of the shaft, wrenching at the cables, trying vainly to shake the killer loose. *I've got to stop him, he's so close. Now he's turning, aiming the gun. . . .*

He saw the killer's frightened face one last time, and below the face the deadly round hole of the gun muzzle, just inches away. A tightening finger, a horrible flash straight in the eyes—

*Dad!*

The thoughts screamed through his mind, one last searing wave of bitterness and hate . . . and then the thoughts snuffed out like a candle, leaving darkness. . . .

*Dad! No! I can't feel you any more . . . what have they done to you? Oh, please, Dad, talk to me again . . . talk to me . . . talk to me. . . .*

IV

DIMLY HE was aware of Dr. Schiml hovering over him, checking his vital signs. Jeff lay very still, hardly even breathing. He felt numb, pummeled beyond description; he did not even want to acknowledge to Schiml that he was alive.

After a moment the doctor turned away. "We can't go

on yet," Jeff heard him say. "We'll have to wait. We're lucky we have him at all, after that."

Across the room, the voice of Paul Conroe, the man who had been creeping down the cables: "Some of that came through to me, even now," he said faintly. "To think that Jeff hated me that much, and *why* he hated me! I never knew about the old man and the son, that they were in full contact like that. If I had known, I never could have done what I did."

The room was still for a long moment. Then Schiml spoke again. "So that was the tremendous power, the mutant strain we've been trying to trace for so long."

"One of the tremendous powers, yes," Conroe said wearily. "Just one of them. Jeff probably has all the power that his father had, buried in his head. It just hasn't fully matured yet. It's latent, waiting for the time that the genes require for fulfillment. Nothing more. He's a living time bomb. And other people have the same powers—hundreds, thousands of other people. Somewhere, a hundred and fifty years ago, there was a change, just a little change in one man or one woman." He paused, and Jeff heard him gather in his breath. "Extrasensory powers, on a galloping scale. It had to be a true mutant strain, an evolutionary step. But it was linked genetically to a sleeper . . . permanently tied to a twisted gene that causes insanity. And a dominant gene, at that. Maybe the change came in just one person, but one became two and two became four or six or eight—extrasensory power and gene-linked insanity. An unholy combination, always linked together, growing together like a cancer. Until now it's eating away the roots of our civilization."

Jeff opened his eyes a slit, saw Conroe get up and cross over to a window. "This answers a great many things, Roger," he was saying. "We knew that old Jacob Meyer had a son. We were even confident that the son would sooner or later develop some of his father's power and probably his psychosis too. But this! None of us in the top levels of government even dreamed it. The father and son were practically two people with one mind, in almost perfect mutual rapport. The son was just so young that he couldn't understand what was wrong. All he knew was that he 'felt' his father and could tell what his father was thinking. Actually, everything that went on in his father's mind, *everything*, was in the boy's mind too, at least during the peaks of the old man's cycle of insanity."

Schiml cut in sharply. "Then there's no doubt that the old man *was* insane?"

"None whatever. He was psychotic, all right. Which was why we were concerned with him in the first place. In those days it was my department in the government —the Department of Statistics—that was supposed to grapple with the problem of the climbing insanity rate you Hoffman Center boys forced us to face up to. And believe me, there was nobody we needed less in that department than a psychotic statistician! Jacob Meyer was insane, all right. He had a regular cycle of elation and depression, so regular we could almost clock it. He had even spotted the symptoms of the psychosis himself, back in his college days, but of course he didn't know what it meant at that time. All he knew was that at certain times he seemed to be surrounded by these peculiar phenomena, which happened rapidly and regularly when he was feeling elated, on top of the world. At other times he seemed to carry an aura of depression along with him. Actually, when he hit the blackest depths of his depressions, he would be bringing about whole strings of disasters to others all around him—suicides, accidents, ill-judged decisions, irrevocable emotional outbursts—all sorts of things. They didn't happen to *him*, of course, just to other people who happened to have the bad luck to be near him." Conroe paused. "Well, we knew all this at the time. What we didn't know was that the man had been looking for the answer himself, *actively searching* for a way to control what he was doing. Nor did we know that it was going to get rapidly worse and worse. We thought we had time to work, time to study. That's why we brought you in on it. And then we discovered that we'd fooled around too long, that right under our noses Jacob Meyer had blossomed into the most dangerous man alive. It was too late then to help him; he simply had to be destroyed before he tore down the whole economic structure of the country single-handed."

"And you were sure that his destructive use of his power was a direct result of the insanity?"

Conroe hesitated. "Not quite," he said thoughtfully. "Actually, you couldn't say that Jacob Meyer 'used' his extrasensory powers at all. They weren't for the most part the kind of powers he could either control or 'use'. They were to sort of powers that just *made things happen*, spontaneously. When he was running high, in a period of elation, or in a deep depression, he made things happen all over the place. The more severe his psychosis became, the more viciously dangerous the things that happened became." Conroe stopped. Jeff felt the man's eyes on him from across the room. "The hellish part of it was that nobody even suspected that the things that happened could possibly be connected up with a human power at all. After all, how could *one human being* have an overwhelming effect on the progress of a whole business cycle? He couldn't, of course, unless he were a dictator, or a tremendously powerful person in some other field. Jacob Meyer was neither. He was just a simple, half-starved statistician with a flock of weird ideas that he couldn't even understand himself but insisted upon publishing in the journals just the same. The university kept him around as a sort of an intellectual gadfly; certainly nobody took him seriously. Or another example: how could one man, just by being in the vicinity, tip the balance that topples the stock market into a three-week panic? Old Meyer wouldn't have believed it himself, although he piled up a rather staggering fortune in profits from stock market fluctuations that he himself was unwittingly bringing about!"

Again Conroe paused. "No, Jacob Meyer's psychokinesis was not the sort of telekinesis that we saw his son Jeff turn against me a few hours ago. The father could probably have managed that, too, if he had hated me enough, but that wouldn't have mattered. If Jacob Meyer's mind had merely affected *physical* things —the turn of a card, the fall of dice, the movement of molecules from one place to another—he would have been a simple problem. We could have isolated him, studied him, maybe helped him. But it wasn't that simple."

The room was quiet for a moment. Then Schiml said, "It seems to me you would have had trouble making your charges stand up in a court of law."

"Trouble! It would have been impossible. We knew it. The government knew it. We had to go outside the law, but we had to destroy the man somehow. *Because Jacob Meyer's mind affected probabilities.* By his very presence he upset the normal probabilities of occurrences going on around him. We watched him, Roger. It was incredible. We watched him in the stock market, and we saw the panic start almost the moment he walked in. We saw eager buyers suddenly change their minds and start selling and then wonder whatever made them do it. We saw what happened at the Bank of the Metropolis that first day we tried to grab him. He was scared, his mind hit a peak of anger and fear, and a bank run started that nearly closed down the most powerful financial house in the world! We saw this one man's *personal, individual effect* on international diplomacy, on finance, on gambling in Las Vegas, on the thinking and behavior of the people around him on the street. It was incredible, Roger."

"But surely Jacob Meyer wasn't the only one."

"There were others, certainly. We know that better

now than we did then. There were and are thousands of them at large, all carrying some degree of extrasensory power from that original mutant strain, all with the gene-linked insanity snarled up with it. We've seen our civilization struggling just to keep on its feet in the face of those thousands. But Jacob Meyer was the first example we'd ever found of the whole, full-blown change in one man. And he was running wild, with his extrasensory powers so firmly enmeshed in his psychosis that there was no hope of separating the two. Meyer tipped us off and put us on the trail, at least. And the trail led to his son after he was dead."

"Yes, the son," Schiml said. "We have the son. We should have had him here long ago."

"Of course we should have, but the son vanished after his father's death. We didn't know where he had gone for years. Then we found out he had spent almost a year in a private hospital, never speaking a word, not even moving voluntarily. They had to exercise him, force feed him, an eight-year-old boy. Presently he pulled out of it, and a couple at the hospital, Em and Barney Trimble took him as a foster son. But we didn't know any of that until the computers picked up an ID on him when he applied for college. Even more important, we didn't know *why* he dropped out of sight like that. Now we know that when we destroyed his father we almost blew our last chance to pin this thing down and study it before it was too late. Because when we killed his father, we killed the son as well."

Schiml snorted. "I don't follow you. He's still alive, he's lying right over there on that table. What's more, he happens to be listening to every word we're saying, in case you didn't know."

"I know that," Conroe said. "And of course he's still alive. But can't you see what *happened* to him? He was a child living in contact with his father's mind. He knew everything his father knew. He just didn't understand it. He thought with his father's thoughts, saw through his father's eyes, because they were mutually and completely telepathic. He felt his father's fear and frustration and bitterness when we finally trapped him in that office building. His body was out on their farm that day, but actually, he was living in his father's mind. It was a mad mind, a mind rising to the screaming heights of mania as he waited for me to come down and kill him, and Jeff was there too, surrounded by his father's hatred. He saw my face through his father's eyes, and all he could understand was that his daddy was being murdered and that I was the one who was murdering him. When the bullet struck, Jeff felt that too. When his father died, Jeff died too, or a part of him did, because they were one mind, and part of that one mind had been destroyed."

Conroe paused. The room was silent except for the sound of Jeff's breathing. Jeff listened numbly, fighting to assimilate what he had heard. "No wonder the boy disappeared!" Conroe went on. "He'd been shot through the head. He was almost literally dead. Maybe he thought he was—I don't know. He must have had good care to pull out of that kind of a shock in a matter of just a year. No wonder we couldn't find a trace of him. Then when he recovered, all he could remember at all was that his father had died. He didn't know how, he didn't know why, and he never dared to remember the truth, because the truth was that he had been killed. All he dared to recognize was my face in recurrent dreams and nightmares."

"But you kept looking for him."

"Oh, yes, I was hunting like mad. I knew that sooner or later I'd find him. But when I ran into him face to face on the library steps of that campus, I was hit with such a blast that I couldn't even tell what he looked like. I couldn't do anything but run. When he saw my face that day, he took complete leave of his senses. He exploded into hatred and bitterness. He knew that I'd killed his father and resolved to hunt me down."

Conroe spread his hands. "It seemed good sense to use that singleness of purpose first to observe him for a while, and then to draw him here. But it was torment for me. He followed me with his mind without even knowing it. I couldn't understand, then, why it seemed to be old Jacob Meyer who came back to haunt me. Because I didn't realize that Jeff had been part of his father's mind when he died, and Jeff didn't know that he was broadcasting that horror whenever he was near me."

Conroe leaned back in his chair, wearily. "We needed Jeff desperately. We needed him *in here,* for testing and then for this study. It's been a long, tedious job getting him here. We still don't know if it's safe—he could be more fearfully dangerous than his father ever was. But at least we have a chance. Left alone, he'll become as insane as his father. There are hundreds, thousands like him, all ESP's, all insane or going insane. But if we can find a way to separate the insanity from the extrasensory powers, we can save them all. If we can't find a way, the government already has its plans made. It have no other choice."

"Choice?" Schiml said.

"But to kill them all, every one. To hunt out the mutant strain and wipe it off the earth so completely that all traces are gone. And to wipe out at the same time the first evolutionary giant-step Man has taken since the dawn of history."

Slowly Roger Schiml stood up. Jeff saw him walk toward the bed. "There's no other possible way?" he asked Conroe.

"None," Conroe said.

"Then I hope Jeff has heard us well. Because it's going to be up to him."

## V

"JEFF," DR. SCHIML was saying. "Jeff Meyer."

Jeff opened his eyes and saw the doctor's face looking down. They had let him sleep for a while, he didn't know how long, but now he was awake again. Awake and back into the nightmare again. He groaned.

"Jeff. You've got to hear me a minute. Listen, Jeff, you've heard it all, before. You know we're trying to help you. And we need your help."

Jeff nodded weakly.

"You know about your father now, the *truth* about your father, don't you?"

"Yes, I know."

"And you want to help?"

"Yes. I have to."

The doctor nodded. "Then you've got to tell us what to do. You have good powers here in your mind, and you also have terrible, ruinous powers. We've got to find them both, find where in your brain they lie, how they work. You'll have to tell us, as we probe, when we strike the good, when we strike the bad. Do you understand, Jeff?"

Again Jeff nodded. He felt infinitely tired. "Go on, Doc. Let's get it over with."

Dr. Schiml reached for the probe controls, moved a dial on the microvernier, moved it again, watching, then moved it still again. And then Jeff didn't know what the doctor did because, abruptly, he was back in the whirlpool. His last thought was that what they were attempting to do now was impossible, and yet somehow it had to succeed.

## VI

HE WAS spinning like a top, end over end, as though he had sprung off a huge, powerful diving board. He rose, still spinning, higher and higher. Jeff knew that his body was still on the soft bed, yet he felt his feet rising, his head sinking, as he spun head over heels through the blackness. And he could feel the tiny probing needle, seeking, hunting, stimulating. . . .

A siren noise broke into his ears, a blast of sound that sent cold shivers down his spine, then leveled off to an up-and-down whine that gradually became almost musical. Somewhere, out of the sound, a voice began whispering in his ear and he paused, straining to hear the words. He knew there were no voices outside his body, he was sure of that, yet he heard this one deep in his ear, first loud, then soft, then louder again, whispering to him. An urgent voice; suddenly it seemed vitally important to hear what it was saying. He shifted slightly and listened harder, until the words came through clearly. . . .

And then he gasped as panic swept through him. They were nonsense words, sounds without meanings. Something stirred in his mind, some vague memory of nonsense words, of a horrible shock . . . had there been a shock? . . . he couldn't remember. But the strange sounds frightened him, driving fear down through the marrow of his bones. They were sinister, babbling sounds, words that *needed* meaning, and had none: half-words that were garbled, twisted, meaningless.

Cautiously he opened his eyes, searching for the whispers in the murky blackness. Some distance away were two shapeless forms, tall and ghostly in black robes

with hoods drawn up over their faces. They were leaning on their sticks, heads together, babbling nonsense to
each other with such fierce earnestness that it seemed
somehow horridly ridiculous. Fighting down panic, Jeff
started toward the two figures.

Then he stopped short.

The moment he had moved, the figures turned sharply toward him, and their nonsense words suddenly became clear for a brief moment: "Stay away, Jeff Meyer.
*Stay away.*"

He stared about him, trembling, trying to orient himself. The hooded figures turned back to each other and
began babbling nonsense again. But now they seemed
to be standing before an archway, guarding it. Slowly,
slyly, Jeff started to move away from them, watching
them with stealthy eyes. As he moved away the murki-
ness seemed to clear and things became brighter. There
was singing in his ears, happy voices, and a great feeling of relief and complacency settled over him like a
mantle. He smiled, and breathed deeper, and started
to roll over for sleep. . . .

*"What was that, Jeff? What did we strike?"*

He shook his head, violently, a frown creasing his
face. "Stay away," he muttered. "The old men, they
were there." Suddenly he felt himself being twisted
around until he was facing the hooded figures again,
and his feet were moving him toward them again, involuntarily, inexorably. Once more the nonsense words
took on meaning, louder than before, and even more
menacing: "No closer, Jeff Meyer, stay away—away—
away."

"Can't go there," he muttered aloud.

*"Why not, Jeff?"*

"They won't let me, I've got to stay away."

*"What are they guarding, Jeff?"*

"I don't know, I don't know, I tell you. I've got to
stay away!"

Suddenly the singing dissolved into a hideous cacophony of clashing sounds, a din that nearly deafened him. A huge wave swept up around him, like a breaker at the ocean's edge, picking him up and hurling him head over heels down a long, whirling tunnel. Desperately he fought for balance, finally found his feet under him once again, but then the ground itself was moving. He ran, frantically, until his breath was coming in short gasps; then he caught a branch of a tree that passed by, and raised himself up as the flooding water swept underneath him. The sky around him was growing black with clouds. In the distance he saw a blinding flash of lightning, ripping through the sky, painting the bleak, wind-torn landscape in sharp relief in his mind as he clung to the branch. He heard a flapping of wings as a huge vulture skimmed by. Then the rain began to fall, a cold, soaking rain that ate through his clothes and soaked his skin, running in torrents into his eyes and ears and mouth.

There were voices all around him. How could there be voices *here?* There were no people, no sign of warm-blooded life here. But he heard the voices, pleasant and musical, all around him. He could see no one, but he could *feel* them.

*Feel them!* he gasped in pure joy, reaching out with his mind, eagerly, unbelievingly, searching out the sudden feeling of perfect, warm *contact* he had just felt. And then his mind was running from person to person, dozens of persons, and he could *feel them all as clearly, as wondrously as he had ever felt his father:* sharply, beautifully.

He cried out then, cried out for joy, tears of unrelieved happiness rolling down his cheeks as he stretched out his mind, embracing the thoughts of the people he could feel but could not see. He felt his own thoughts being met, embraced, *understood.* "Right here!" he he shouted. "Schiml, this is it, don't lose it! This is the center. I'm controlling it. You've got it now. *Work it, Schiml, work it for all you're worth!*"

He looked at the black, menacing sky around him, and his mind laughed and cried out for the clouds to go away. There was a wild whirling of clouds, and they broke, and the sun was streaming down on him. He threw himself from the tree, ran down the hillside, free, with a huge, wonderful, overpowering freedom he had never felt before, his mind free to soar and soar without hindrance, with nothing now to stand between it and complete understanding of other men. A mind which could go wherever he wanted it to go, to do whatever he wished. He ran down toward the bottom of the hill, feeling his control growing with every step he took. He knew when he reached the bottom of the hill the battle would be won, so he ran faster.

Suddenly, like some horrible nightmare, the hooded figures loomed up directly in his path, long bony fingers stabbing out at him accusingly. He stopped short at the overpowering warning in the voices that came out to meet him. He stood there, looking at the hooded ones, sobbing. He felt spent, beaten, and he wept bitterly and hopelessly as the dark clouds gathered again. He was too late, too late.

"*What are they guarding, Jeff?*"

"I don't know, I don't know. I can't break through—"

"*You've got to, Jeff. You mustn't stop now. We've got the extrasensory center, that was it back there, but something is blocking it. Something is keeping you away, Jeff. You've got to see what—*"

"I can't. Oh, I can't. Please don't make me!"

"*You must, Jeff!*"

"No!"

"*Go on, Jeff—*"

He stood up, facing the hooded figures, cowering, his whole body trembling. Deep in his mind he could feel the probing needle, moving, slowly moving, forcing him nearer and nearer to the grim figures. Slowly his feet moved, dragging in the face of a paralyzing fear that demanded every ounce of strength he possessed just to make his legs function. And the voices, heavy with menace, were grating in his ear, "Stay out, stay away. If you want to live, stay away—away—away. . . ."

He moved closer and closer to the hooded figures, leaned forward to peer around them toward the gray, ghastly gate they guarded, a gate heavy with mold, with rusty iron braces.

And then he reached up and threw back the hood of the first figure, stared at the face it had concealed. *It was his own face.*

He turned to the other, peered intently, fighting to see the face before the features blurred out beyond recognition. It was his face, too, unmistakably. With a roar of anger and frustration he tore away the hoods, ripped them off, one with each hand, and stripped off the concealing shrouds.

He had been guarding the gate himself, for the figures were mere skeletons with his face. He struck at them and they shattered like thin glass, falling down in pieces at his feet. He brushed his feet through the debris and pressed his shoulder against the gate, heaving against it until it swung open. Creaking on rusty hinges, it swung open . . . *into a place of madness.*

He screamed twice, short, frantic screams, as he tried to hide his eyes from the writhing horror behind the gate. "Here!" he cried out to Schiml. "It's here! "You're at the right place, this is what you're looking for. Cut it away, destroy it before we lose it. Please, I can't stand it any longer."

His feet moved through the horrible gate, into the swarming, loathsome, horror-ridden madness that lay beyond, and he screamed again as he saw the bright flash, felt the wrenching, sickening lurch that hurled him to the ground. There was pain then, and blackness, then another blinding flash. He felt his muscles collapse, and his mind collapse, and he fell and lay helpless. As on the day when he had died once before, he felt his mind fade away like vapor in the sun.

## VII

WHEN HE opened his eyes, he saw Paul Conroe's face. He went tense for a moment, every muscle going into spasm. Then he relaxed, blinking, and stared up at Conroe in bewilderment. Somehow, he didn't hate Conroe any more.

"I'm sorry, Jeff," Conroe was saying. "I don't know the words to tell you how sorry I am." There were tears in Conroe's eyes, and Jeff looked at him and felt a strange, blossoming sense of wonder. For Conroe had stopped talking and yet he *knew* what Conroe was trying to say. He shook his head slowly. "Don't worry," he said softly. "That kind of word doesn't exist. You don't need words for that."

"And you feel all right?"

"Yes." And then: "I—I'm alive!" Jeff struggled to sit up as a twinge of pain shot down his spine.

Schiml was there in an instant, gently easing him back. "Easy there, you're alive, all right. And you're well. And there's no irony in calling you a Mercy Man." His eyes gleamed in happy triumph. "You're a whole human being, Jeff—the way you were intended to be— for the first time in your life."

The words came to him clearly enough, yet Jeff knew that not a single word had actually been spoken. "Just like my father," he murmured. "I just felt him, knew what he was thinking."

Tears were running down Schiml's cheeks; he seemed like an infinitely happy small boy, beside himself. He raised a finger and pointed to the glass on the table near the bed. He looked at Jeff. "Make it move, lad. You can, you know."

Jeff stared at the glass. It shifted, then rose slowly two inches off the table and hung suspended there, glowing slightly in the dim light of the room. Then, gently, it floated back to the table. "Control," Jeff said softly. "I have control."

"The power was chained down to something else, before," Schiml said. "You had the extrasensory power, yes, but it was linked to something that would have prevented you from ever gaining control. A degenerative insanity, part and parcel of the extrasensory power. You're not alone, Jeff—there are many hundreds like you, in greater or lesser degrees. Conroe is like you, to a very limited extent. And he's been trying to find a way to separate the two, for years. So have I. That's why you're *really* a Mercy Man. Without what you did, thousands would have had to die. We knew there were two centers, but we knew no way to separate them. We had to have you to guide us. We had to find the center of insanity in your brain and destroy it without destroying the other, without destroying you. That's what we've waited twenty years for. You're free of it now. The insanity is gone. And now we have a technique we can use to free a thousand others like you."

Jeff stared about him, wonderingly. Sunlight came streaming in the window. They had moved him high up in one of the ward towers for recovery. Across the way, he could see another of the ward towers of the Hoffman Medical Center, white and gleaming in the sunlight. He took a deep breath of the fresh air and turned again to the two men standing by the bedside. "Then it *was* you who were hunting me," he murmured. "Strange, isn't it? It wasn't me hunting Conroe. It was my father, or the ghost of my father, still there in my mind. The ghost of a sick man's mind." His eyes narrowed, and he looked up at Schiml. "Then there were others who knew, too. Blackie knew. She *must* have been the girl in the nightclub."

"She was. A little heavy makeup, a little light plastic,

those changed her enough to deceive you. But she never even knew she was there. Hypnosis can be powerful, and it can erase all memory." He paused, smiling at Jeff. "Blackie will be the next one for treatment. We need her so much in the work we have to do here, almost as much as we need you. But you've freed Blackie, too. She'll be happier than she's ever been since her mind started broadcasting bad luck to everyone around her, back fifteen years ago. She'll be happier by far."

Much later he awoke and saw her sitting quietly across the room, watching the fading evening light as the sun began to set. When she saw he was awake, she crossed the room, and took his hand. "I was so afraid, so terribly afraid."

"Do you still want to leave?" he asked.

"Oh, no—not now. No, there's too much to do." She stared at him, startled. "Do you?"

He didn't answer for a moment. *"You can go, if you want to,"* Paul Conroe had said before he left. *"Or you can stay, whichever you choose. If you go we won't try to stop you, nor blame you. But we really need you."*

There would be others staying too, of course. The Nasty Frenchman would stay, sneering, laughing, conspiring, always aiming at the big money that forever lurked in the future, completely unaware of the real errand of mercy he was running with his life. And Harpo would stay, and all the others.

Including Blackie. Poor, helpless Blackie, beautiful, bitter, desperate. For her there would be a new lease. And there was no way of telling the person she would be after the new lease was signed.

He grinned up at her. "Tell you what," he said. "Maybe when it's all over, when they're through with us and the work is really done, then maybe we can go away. Out to the West Coast, anywhere. You and me and a set of dice."

And they laughed at that, and at other things. Weary as he was, they laughed and talked and planned far into the night.

# BEST-SELLING
## *Science Fiction*
### *and*
## *Fantasy*

| | | |
|---|---|---|
| ☐ 47809-3 | **THE LEFT HAND OF DARKNESS,** Ursula K. LeGuin $2.95 | |
| ☐ 16012-3 | **DORSAI!,** Gordon R. Dickson $2.75 | |
| ☐ 80581-7 | **THIEVES' WORLD,** Robert Lynn Asprin, editor $2.95 | |
| ☐ 11577-2 | **CONAN #1,** Robert E. Howard, L. Sprague de Camp, Lin Carter $2.50 | |
| ☐ 49142-1 | **LORD DARCY INVESTIGATES,** Randall Garrett $2.75 | |
| ☐ 21889-X | **EXPANDED UNIVERSE,** Robert A. Heinlein $3.95 | |
| ☐ 87328-6 | **THE WARLOCK UNLOCKED,** Christopher Stasheff $2.95 | |
| ☐ 10253-0 | **CHANGELING,** Roger Zelazny $2.95 | |
| ☐ 05469-2 | **BERSERKER,** Fred Saberhagen $2.75 | |
| ☐ 51552-5 | **THE MAGIC GOES AWAY,** Larry Niven $2.75 | |

# MORE SCIENCE FICTION!
## ADVENTURE

# THE CHILDE CYCLE SERIES

## By Gordon R. Dickson

| | | |
|---|---|---|
| ☐ 16012-3 | **DORSAI!** | $2.75 |
| ☐ 49300-9 | **LOST DORSAI** | $2.95 |
| ☐ 56854-8 | **NECROMANCER** | $2.75 |
| ☐ 77420-2 | **SOLDIER, ASK NOT** | $2.75 |
| ☐ 77804-6 | **SPIRIT OF DORSAI** | $2.75 |
| ☐ 79972-8 | **TACTICS OF MISTAKE** | $2.50 |

*Available at your local bookstore or return this form to:*